Diary of a
6th Grade
NINJA

Buchanan Bandits

Diary of a 6th Grade NINJA

BOOK 6
Buchanan Bandits

MARCUS EMERSON

ILLUSTRATED BY **DAVID LEE**

ALLEN&UNWIN
SYDNEY • MELBOURNE • AUCKLAND • LONDON

First published by Allen & Unwin in 2017

Allen & Unwin
83 Alexander Street
Crows Nest NSW 2065
Australia
Phone: (61 2) 8425 0100
Email: info@allenandunwin.com
Web: www.allenandunwin.com

A Cataloguing-in-Publication entry is available
from the National Library of Australia
www.trove.nla.gov.au

ISBN 978 1 76029 560 8

Cover design by Marcus Emerson and Sandra Nobes
Text design by Sandra Nobes
Cover and internal illustrations by David Lee
Set in 14 pt Adobe Garamond by Sandra Nobes
Printed in Australia by SOS Print + Media Group

10 9 8

www.marcusemerson.com

This one's for Parker ...

STARRING
- CHASE (ME)
- ZOE
- GAVIN
- FAITH
- BRAYDEN
- NAOMI
w/special appearances by
Aliens & James Buchanan!

ALSO STARRING
- WYATT
- SEBASTIAN
- JAKE & THE WOLFPACK
- OLIVE
w/special appearances by
The Library Zombies!

There comes a point in everyone's life when they find themselves getting chased by a pack of ferocious werewolves. But I didn't think it would happen to me until I was much older, like in *seventh* grade.

My name is Chase Cooper, and I'm a sixth grade ninja... getting chased by werewolves.

I sprinted through the dark forest. Branches slapped at my face as if they were against the idea of my escape. I'm not sure what I did to make the trees angry. Maybe it was because I carved my initials into one of their friends when I was younger – who knows?

I pulled my ninja mask from the hood of my sweatshirt and slipped it over my face.

THAT'S ME →
CHASE COOPER
(NINJA EXTRAORDINAIRE)

With every step, dry leaves crunched under my feet. I could hear the same crunching from behind me. The monsters were closing in and I knew there wasn't much time until they caught me.

'Man, Chase is really out,' a werewolf said.

2

I wasn't sure what the monster meant by that, but I didn't want to find out.

'Draw something on his face,' another werewolf giggled.

The other monsters chuckled with her.

Panic washed over me, so I tried running faster but it felt like my feet were sinking in mud. I was still moving, but it was like someone had hit the slow-motion button on me. Since escape wasn't an option anymore, I spun around, ready to face the werewolves.

As their growls grew louder, I clenched my fists. There was no way this ninja was going to go out like this.

Suddenly the werewolves burst through the trees like violent water crashing against the shoreline. I braced myself for impact, setting my feet firmly in the ground, expecting a collision of epic proportions.

But instead I felt an explosion of hot air come from behind me. The blast was so strong that the surrounding trees face planted, flattening the werewolves into the earth like mushrooms being squashed by that little plumber guy in that video game. I watched as the furry monsters blinked rapidly and then burst into a thousand tiny drops of light, fading out of existence.

It was *super* cool.

'*Chase Cooper!*' boomed a voice from the sky.

I turned slowly to face my enemy, afraid. I had a pretty good idea what I was going to see. Crossing my fingers, I whispered, 'Please don't be a giant robot monster of President James

ROBOT PRESIDENT JAMES BUCHANAN

ME →

Buchanan. *Please* don't be a giant robot monster of President James Buchanan! *Please!'*

But of course, standing before me, nearly fifteen metres tall, was a *giant robot monster of President James Buchanan*... and he looked angry.

The robot raised one foot slowly and slammed it into the ground as he took a step forward. Everything shook as he laughed heartily, arching his head back like an evil villain.

As the robot's head sailed forward, I got a good look into his eyes, and saw exactly the kind of evil necessary to create this massive robot of destruction. It was Wyatt, leader of the red ninja clan.

He was pulling on levers and pushing buttons inside one of the eyes of the robot like he was handling some kind of oversized video game controller.

WYATT

A bunch of red ninjas teleported into existence around the robot's feet and started rushing towards me with drawn swords.

I smirked, remembering my ninja training. I stepped forwards and clapped my hands together as powerfully as I could, releasing a sonic boom of super sub-zero temperatures that turned the red ninjas into frozen popsicles.

Don't ask me how it was done – it's a top-secret ninja move that involves crazy science ... or something.

Suddenly, a voice cut through the air, squealing in fear. '*Help!*'

My eyes narrowed, quickly scanning the
monster until I saw the source of the plea. It
was my friend Faith! She was being held captive
in the left hand of the robot. His grip must've
been strong
because she was
struggling to free
herself from it.

FAITH

GIANT
ROBOT
HAND

'Faith! Hang
on, I'm coming!'
I shouted.

I leapt through
the air, straight
for President
Buchanan's robot
face. The air behind
me caught fire from how quickly I was flying
through space. I stuck out my fist, aiming for
the robot's eye where Wyatt was comfortably
sitting, probably sipping on soft drink with a
mouth full of snacks.

'*Wyaaaaaaaaaatt!*' was my battle cry as I shot
forward.

'*Chase!*' Faith shouted. '*Look out for his other hand!*'

But it was too late. I was too focused on making it to Wyatt that I totally ignored the rest of the robot's body. President Buchanan's mighty robotic hand was the last thing I saw before it swatted me like a bug.

Instantly, my head snapped up. My arms shot forward as I struggled to catch myself before falling into the dark forest below me, which ... wasn't there anymore. Instead of trees, I saw a cold linoleum floor. And instead of falling to my death, I was sitting on a bench. I looked up and blinked slowly, soaking in all the information I could. A pink eraser was staring back at me.

... and so were all my friends.

◆ ◆ ◆

Students devoured their food at cafeteria tables across the room. It was lunchtime on Monday. I was always extra tired on Mondays and have been known to drift off during class from time

8

GAVIN FAITH ME ZOE BRAYDEN

to time. I patted at the pocket of my jeans, making sure my phone didn't fall out when I jumped awake. I was happy to see that it was still there.

'Good morning, sunshine!' Zoe, my cousin, said as she grabbed the eraser from the table. Zoe's one of the nicest, coolest kids on this planet. Even if she weren't my cousin, I think I'd still be friends with her, and that's saying a lot.

I rubbed the sore spot on my head, still too confused to talk. A small puddle of drool was left on the table where my face had been, and I could feel that my cheek was wet. Embarrassed, I dug my chin into my shoulder, trying to wipe the drool away, but only made it worse by smearing it all over my shirt.

'*Sick*,' Gavin laughed. Gavin used to be the captain of the hall monitors. He's a serious dude, and was crucial in busting the kids responsible for wreaking havoc at the talent show awhile back. He's also going out with Zoe, which is ... yuck.

Everyone else laughed with Gavin. I knew my friends weren't actually making fun of me, but I was still embarrassed.

'What the *heck* were you dreaming about?' Zoe asked, smiling like she knew a secret.

I tripped over my words until I finally managed to form a sentence. 'I, uh, it was nothing ... really, it wasn't. Just something about werewolves and robot presidents controlled by a wavy-haired kid.'

Zoe tilted her head slightly, still grinning. 'Was *Faith* in the dream?'

Faith sat across the table, covering her mouth. Faith is *super* awesome. She's the only girl I know who actually *wants* to play zombie video games. One time she brought over a pizza for lunch and we spent the afternoon playing ranked matches online. I went up at least ten levels with her on my team!

'Great,' I murmured. 'Was I talking in my sleep again?'

'*Mumbling* is more like it. You *might've* said something about rescuing Faith at one point,' Brayden said. Brayden was one of the first kids I became friends with a Buchanan. He's a wealth of knowledge when it comes to monsters and is obsessed with werewolves, which is probably why they were in my dream.

Everyone laughed at Brayden's comment, even Faith, which helped me feel less embarrassed. If she had acted weird, then it would've been awkward, but since she was in on the joke, it was cool. I couldn't help but laugh a little myself.

'I always have weird dreams when I eat gummy bears before I go to sleep,' I said, and then added, 'And I had, like, *a lot*. There's an irresponsible amount of gummy bears in my belly right now.'

'Bad dreams are the worst,' Zoe commented.

'Bad dream? More like one of the most *awesome* dreams I've ever had!' I said, rubbing the sore spot on my noggin again. 'Did one of you guys flick my head or something?'

Zoe held out the pink block eraser so I could see it. 'I think Jake threw it.'

Jake was seated at the table right behind ours. He spun around on his seat when he heard his name. 'Enjoy your nap, little baby?'

JAKE

Jake was easily one of the 'coolest' kids at Buchanan, but that didn't make him cool by any means. He was one of the tough guys, always picking on someone to make himself look awesome. As the star quarterback, all of the football team respected him, following him around like a wolf pack.

To put it bluntly, Jake was a jerk.

Jake had targeted me ever since I switched the school's mascot from a wildcat to a moose. Long story short – a few months ago I was given the opportunity to choose a new school mascot. After a lot of thought, I chose the moose because those things are massive and majestic. Of course *now* I see how uncool a moose can be, but at the time I seriously thought I was doing something great!

A lot of kids were annoyed with my decision, but Jake took it personally since he was a rock star on the football team.

I wiped my mouth again, hoping there wasn't any more drool on my face.

'Go ahead and *keep* that eraser,' Jake laughed. 'I got a million of 'em!'

As always, I wanted to say something mean to him but just couldn't bring myself to do it. 'Thanks, man. That's very generous of you!'

'Nice burn,' Faith muttered.

Before I could say anything else, the bell above the stage went off, signalling the end of lunch. If this were a normal week, then

13

everyone would dump their trays and filter out of the cafeteria to class, but this week was different.

It was the sixth graders' careers week.

The last half of each day was going to be spent in the cafeteria, learning about all kinds of different careers. It was a way for us to gain some real-world experience *way* before venturing out into the real world ourselves.

I'm normally against stuff like this because it feels a little forced, but in this case, I was really excited. Each student would be paired with a professional from the career they chose, and they would learn about it throughout the rest of the week. A careers fair, which was basically a huge party, would be held on Friday afternoon.

I'm pretty sure it's the teachers' way of rewarding themselves for a stressful week of students crammed into a cafeteria.

The school president, Sebastian, was the student in charge of the entire event. I know what you're thinking – if Sebastian is in charge of it, it *must* be shady.

For those who are new to the story, allow me to quickly explain what I've had to deal with since my first day at Buchanan School.

It's pretty much all to do with a kid named Wyatt who, I'm sure you remember, was piloting the robot President Buchanan. During the first week of school, Wyatt recruited me into his ninja clan. Some bad stuff went down and I ended up leading the ninja clan. Ever since then, Wyatt has been a *splinter* in my *eyeball.* He's even recently started referring to me as his 'sworn enemy'.

A few months ago, Wyatt started a second ninja clan that secretly trains in the abandoned greenhouse at the centre of the school. The *red* ninja clan. They all wear red wristbands so they can tell each other apart when they're not in their ninja robes.

President Sebastian and Wyatt are now BFFs or something because Sebastian made Wyatt the hall monitor captain, *firing* Gavin from that position.

It was possible that up until that point, Sebastian was just picking bad friends, but I soon found out that there was more going on than anyone realised. It was only last week that Gavin and I saw Sebastian hanging out with Wyatt *in* the greenhouse while the red ninjas trained.

Oh yeah, and get this – Wyatt's now the school's vice president. Last week, a penguin named Hotcakes was lost in the school and I'm the one who found him, but *Wyatt's* the one who got credit for it. And what happened because of that? Sebastian made him VP right there on the spot. Everyone was so happy that Hotcakes was safe that they cheered at Wyatt's promotion.

Those last four paragraphs would be the strangest thing I've ever written if they weren't the truth. What a school, huh?

President Sebastian is clearly in cahoots with Wyatt, but I had no idea why.

Anyway, the career week was Sebastian's idea, and Principal Davis loved it so much that he ran with it. To be honest, everyone thought it was a great idea. Every student in the school was stoked to be a part of it, me included, which is how I found myself standing over a cafeteria table that had a name tag with 'Chase Cooper' on it.

My table was next to the school supply shop, which was called 'the Pit'. Teachers call it the Pit because it was like the pit stop in those car races, where cars stop to refuel and get repaired. They thought the supply shop was like that for kids, since we buy school supplies and snacks from there.

But the *students* called it the Pit because it was in a part of the cafeteria that stunk like an armpit, in the far corner of the lunchroom, near the exit that led to the school dumpsters. The smell was horrendous, especially on hot days. There were times that it stunk so bad it gave me a headache.

I pinched the clip on the back of my name tag and attached it to my shirt. Under the name tag was a folder with some sheets of paper tucked inside. I took a seat and flipped open the folder.

There were some pamphlets that explained the job search process and other ones about how pens are made. Is that a common job? Pen making?

'Can I have everyone's attention, please?' Principal Davis said from the front of the cafeteria. He clapped his hands. 'Please everyone, eyes up here.'

The room full of students slowly became silent. I saw Zoe and Faith a few tables down, sitting next to each other. Gavin and Brayden were also seated at another a table together. My shoulders slumped. How come *they* got to sit together?

Principal Davis continued. 'At your table, you'll find your name tags along with a folder of important items you'll need for the week. Please clip your name tags to your shirts so your mentor knows your name.'

I wondered if Principal Davis would have a hard time finding a real ninja to be my mentor. Who am I kidding? *Of course* he'd have a hard time finding one because you don't find a ninja... *they find you.*

'Open your folder and take a look at the last sheet,' Principal Davis said.

The last sheet was a piece of orange and white card with numbers down the front of it. Next to each number was a set of blank circles marked with letters of the alphabet. It looked like a *test*.

'There's a questionnaire for each student to fill out,' Principal Davis said. 'Once you're done, please leave them on the table for a teacher to pick up. The results of your questionnaire will determine which career is right for you, so answer as honestly as you can.'

'*What?*' I whispered hoarsely. 'We don't get to choose our careers?'

From the other side of the table, someone said, 'What? You thought you could just write 'ninja' and one would show up to this school?'

I didn't need to turn around to know it was Wyatt. And judging from the smell of spearmint, I was pretty sure his girlfriend, Olivia Jones, was right next to him. They're the weirdest couple I'd ever seen. Most of the time, they just stand in the hallway between classes, holding hands and laughing maniacally. Imagine that for a second. Weird, right?

'*Aloha,*' Wyatt grinned when I finally looked at him. I'm not sure why he said hello in Hawaiian. He's definitely not from Hawaii.

Wyatt was wearing a sash with 'VICE PRESIDENT' on it. I'm pretty sure the school doesn't have a sash like that, which means that Wyatt probably made it himself.

I nodded once just to acknowledge his presence. Next to him, Olive was chomping away on chewing gum like she was *trying* to be

annoying. She
had so much gum in her
mouth that she could barely chew with her
mouth closed! If she wasn't chewing so loudly,
I probably would've been impressed.

I looked around, hoping a teacher was
nearby because chewing gum was strictly
forbidden at school. If it gets in the carpet, it's
nearly *impossible* to get out. Unsurprisingly,
there wasn't a teacher in sight.

'Looks like we'll be sitting together this week,'
Wyatt said, smirking.

I opened my mouth to speak, but Wyatt cut
across me in a loud voice.

'Hey, listen,' he said, closing his eyes. 'Now
that I'm the school VP, I think it's safe to say

I'm not going to try anything, okay? You can cool it, turbo.'

I had to literally bite my tongue. If I was going to spend a week next to him, it would probably be best if I didn't say anything I'd regret.

I nodded again at him. 'Deal.'

Nobody else at our table had noticed our short conversation. They were all busy scratching their pencils on the test sheet, filling in circles. Wyatt and Olive had started doing the same. I breathed a sigh of relief. Maybe this week wouldn't be so bad after all.

I scanned the questions and had to laugh at a few of them.

Would you rather a) TRAIN an army of baby kangaroos, or b) FIGHT an army of baby kangaroos?

Would you say you were a) a morning person, b) a night owl, or c) a machine sent back in time to fight the resistance?

If you could fist fight a zombie, would you? a) Yes, or b) No.

22

I know, right? There were a *hundred* of these bizarre questions!

After about twenty minutes of listening to Olive's chewing, I finally finished the test. I flipped it over, spun around on the bench and faced the rest of the room, watching the other students finished their questionnaires as well.

A few kids began walking aimlessly around the cafeteria. It wasn't like there wasn't anything to do. The staff had put up a bunch of work-stations so kids could participate in different activities, which kept most of the kids busy.

I glanced across the room to see what Brayden and Gavin were doing, but they weren't at their table anymore. I finally saw them huddled with some other kids near the centre of the cafeteria. Gavin had his brow furrowed in concern, but I'm pretty sure he always looked like that. It wasn't until I saw Brayden pull the same expression that I knew something was wrong.

I stood up and joined the crowd of students. I was on the outside of the circle, so I couldn't tell what was going on yet.

'What's up?' I asked Brayden.

Brayden shrugged. 'Somebody stole something, I think.'

Gavin leaned over and stood on his tippy toes. 'Not *some*body, *a lot* of bodies. A few kids had some things stolen.'

'Okay,' I said, 'so why isn't anyone speaking up about it? Why the weird huddle of whispers and secrets?'

'Because it was *gum* that was stolen,' Faith said, stepping out of the circle to join our conversation.

Zoe was right behind her. 'Someone stole gum from *ten* kids.'

'Ah,' Brayden sighed. 'So it's not like they'd get help to begin with. They'd be asked why they even had gum in the first place.'

'Exactly,' Faith said, rubbing her arms like she was cold.

'Someone managed to get away with stealing gum from *ten* kids?' I whispered.

Faith nodded. 'It was taken right out of some of their pockets!'

'That's crazy! That's...' I trailed off. I wanted to say it sounded like the work of a ninja.

'What's crazy is that some of these kids said they still had their gum *before* answering the questions on that career test,' Faith added. 'That was only, like, twenty minutes ago.'

Zoe narrowed her eyes at Wyatt as he approached. 'It was *you*, wasn't it?'

'*What* was me?' Wyatt asked, annoyed.

As much as I didn't want to, I knew I had to speak up because it was the honourable thing to do.

'No,' I said, coming to Wyatt's defence. 'He was with me the entire time, before *and* after the career test. He never left my sight.' I pointed at Olive, who was still chomping away. 'She was with him too, so it wasn't her either. Even though it *looks* like she's chewing enough gum for a football team, she was chewing on it before the career test.'

Olive pushed the wad of gum into her cheek and stuck her tongue out at Zoe.

'*Nice*,' Zoe said, disgusted and crinkling her nose.

Wyatt looked over his shoulder. It looked like he was hiding something. Knowing Wyatt, he probably was.

Without saying another word, the leader of the red ninja clan turned and walked away with Olive by his side.

Gavin folded his arms, scowling. He spoke. 'If it were just one kid with the problem, I'd be inclined to ignore it, but since it's *ten* kids, there's a strange pattern goin' on, ain't there?'

'Yeah, we should investigate,' I said.

Zoe immediately chimed in. 'No way! How about just living a normal sixth grader life for once? No mysteries, no clues, no action, no adventure?'

'Right,' I grumbled. 'Because that's a *bajillion* times more fun.'

'Bajillion's not a word,' Zoe snipped.

I lowered my head and mumbled, 'Is too.'

'Is *not*,' Zoe replied.

I paused, sitting in awkward silence for at least five seconds as our friends stood around.

Finally, I whispered quieter than anyone could hear, '*Is too.*'

Gavin raised his hands as if he were giving up. 'Looks like I'm out,' he said. 'It's alright though. It's just a bit of stolen gum.'

Just a bit of stolen gum? Didn't Gavin understand that the item that was stolen wasn't the point? The *point* was that something was *stolen*!

As Zoe and Gavin walked away, the front pocket of my pants vibrated. I jumped, afraid that a bug was crawling up my leg, before I realised it was my phone going off. I looked at the screen to see who the message was from, but it was a number I didn't recognise.

I unlocked my phone and read the message.

Meet me backstage asap. Come alone.
—Wyatt

A girl snickered right next to me. It was Naomi, one of the most devoted members of my ninja clan. 'Yeah, because *that* sounds like a good idea.'

I clicked the button on top of my phone, locking it. Gavin was already on the other side of the room. Brayden was talking with Faith at another table. Naomi was the only one who knew I got a text from Wyatt. Slipping my phone back into my front pocket, I said something that surprised even *me*. 'I think I'm gonna see what he wants.'

Naomi's jaw dropped like a DJ dropping the bass. '*Are you kidding me?*' she cried out.

Everyone nearby looked to see what she had screamed about.

Scratching the back of my head, I faked a laugh and led Naomi aside. When we were away from the nosy students, I said, 'I understand that my history with Wyatt hasn't been the best.'

Naomi folded her arms. 'You win understatement of the year award, congratulations! What do you plan on spending your prize money on?'

I laughed at her sarcasm.

Naomi's face switched from anger to concern.

'You're not seriously going to meet him, are you? He's so... evil!'

I paused for a second. 'I'm just going to see what he wants, is that so bad?'

Naomi's eyes grew fierce. 'I'm going with you.'

'That's not necessary,' I said. 'I'll be fine, really.'

To my surprise, Naomi grabbed my arm and dragged me along with her. 'I saw what he did to you during that first week of school, and I know what he's capable of. You're gonna need a friend if he snaps again.'

'He's *not* gonna snap again,' I said, but an uncomfortable feeling washed over me. What if he *did* snap again? I remembered Wyatt's fist connecting with my face. 'Alright, maybe it's a good idea for you to come.'

Naomi turned her head and smiled. 'Going alone was never an option.'

Monday.
Backstage in the cafeteria.

Naomi and I decided to pull our ninja masks
on when we were out of the sight of the rest of
the students in the cafeteria. Since there was so
much activity going on, none of the teachers
saw us sneak through the heavy velvet stage
curtains.

'After you,' Naomi said, her voice muffled by
her mask. She held her hand out, gesturing
across the dark stage.

I crouched, taking the lead. 'As your ninja
leader, I'd have thought *you'd* want to go first to
make sure everything was clear.'

Naomi laughed. 'Yeah, right. You're not *that* great of a leader.'

'Kay,' I said. 'Just give me a minute. Sometimes when I'm nervous, it helps me to just sit still for a minute and count the seconds.'

Naomi's eyes narrowed. 'Whatever you say.'

I shut my eyes and inhaled deeply. Feeling the muscles in my body relax, I began the countdown. 'One hundred, ninety-nine, ninety-eight, ninety-seven—'

'I thought you only counted a minute!' Naomi hissed.

'I do!' I replied, annoyed by her interruption.

'But you started at a *hundred*!'

'Yeah, a *minute*.'

Naomi glared at me until it finally clicked.

'Oh right,' I said, feeling silly. 'Sixty seconds. Not a hundred.'

Naomi covered her mouth, holding in her laughter.

'Whatever,' I said. 'Let's just go.'

As we approached the back of the stage, I saw a soft red light coming from around the far

corner of the stage, as if it was guiding us, telling us where to go.

When we made it to the centre, I glanced up, studying the curtain that loomed over us.

Naomi read my thoughts. 'You're thinking about the white ninja, aren't you?'

'Mmhmm,' I hummed.

The white ninja had saved me from the red ninjas. The first time, he pulled me up and away from harm when I was getting chased. The second time, he dumped the curtain on a pack of red ninjas during the school's talent show just before they were about to beat the living daylights out of me.

'Do you know who it is?' Naomi asked.

'No idea,' I replied. 'But I think he's on our side.'

'What makes you think that?'

'Because he saved me... *twice*.'

'That's doesn't mean anything,' Naomi grunted. 'Maybe he's playing you, making you think he's on your side.'

'Why would he do that?'

'Who knows?' she answered. 'I just think you should keep your guard up. This school seems to have it out for you.'

'*Right?!*' I said. 'Like President Buchanan is haunting the halls of the school and trying to ruin my life?'

Naomi rolled her eyes. '*Riiiiiiight,*' she sang. 'I'm actually not surprised you believe that.'

We made it to the far side of the stage, where the soft red light turned the corner. Carefully, I stepped down the short staircase and into the small hallway stacked with boxes from the drama club.

As soon as my foot touched the ground, the red light clicked brighter. About three metres away from Naomi and me was an old leather chair, facing away from us. Above the chair was a red light bulb swinging slowly through the air, making the shadows on the floor expand and shrink. There was a weird burning smell in the air and I suddenly felt like a character in an '80s horror movie who'd stupidly walked into a trap.

'This is it,' I whispered, my stomach dropping. 'This is how I die...'

The chair spun around, scaring the spew out of me. I jumped backwards, bumping into Naomi.

'Our fearless leader,' she joked.

The red light bulb flickered a couple of times before switching to a bright white. I squinted, trying to see who was in the chair.

'Dude,' Wyatt said, leaning back in the leather chair. He wasn't wearing his ninja outfit. 'Relax, it's me. I mean, you *knew* it was gonna be me, right? I signed the text message with my name.'

'You didn't have to make it feel like I was walking into a freaky nightmare!' I said.

Wyatt chuckled. 'Right, sorry about that,' he said, pointing at the light. 'That old bulb really needs to be replaced.' He spun in his chair again, raising a hand to someone hiding in the darkness. 'Is it ready yet?'

I thought maybe it was Olive, but it wasn't.

'Almost, sir,' a boy's voice said from the shadows.

I pulled my mask off and tucked it away in the hood of my sweatshirt. 'What is this? What's that smell?'

In answer, a boy wearing a suit stepped out of the shadows, handing Wyatt a porcelain plate. A Belgian waffle sat on it, steaming hot and fresh.

Let me say that again in case you missed it ... *a Belgian waffle.*

'Would you like one?' Wyatt asked, as if getting handed a freshly cooked waffle backstage and in the middle of the school day was a totally normal thing to happen. I guess being vice president had its perks.

The boy in the suit sprayed whipped cream onto the top of Wyatt's waffle. I seriously felt like I was losing my mind. I shook my head, remembering why I was there. 'Why did you text me? *What do you want?*'

Wyatt took a bite. With a cheek full of waffle, he pointed his fork at Naomi and said, 'I *told* you to come alone.'

'You're lucky I'm here at all,' I said.

Wyatt stopped chewing and looked at me, head tilted like a confused dog. 'I'm sorry, what did you say? I couldn't hear you over the sound of my own awesomeness.'

'You mean the sound of you chewing with your mouth fully open?' Naomi said. 'I'm *shocked* no food has fallen out.'

'If you want to talk to me,' I said boldly, 'then Naomi stays.'

Swallowing his bite, Wyatt nodded. 'Fine,' he said. 'Naomi is cool. She's a good ninja. I remember her from when I was the leader of your clan.'

'You mean when you were the leader for, like, less than a week?' Naomi said scornfully. It was obvious that she wasn't afraid of Wyatt, and her little remarks made me feel more comfortable with this whole situation.

'You fool!' Wyatt snapped, like some kind of villain. 'Don't you realise your insults only make me stronger?'

Naomi giggled at Wyatt's little outburst.

Wyatt held out his plate of food as he inhaled slowly, calming himself down. The boy in the suit took it from him, replacing it with a tiny green item.

'I want to call a truce,' Wyatt said as he held it out for me to see. It was a four-leaf clover. 'I assume you remember the first task I ever assigned to you?'

I stared at the clover. 'You said if I wanted to join your ninja clan, I had to return to the hideout with one of those.'

'Exactly,' Wyatt nodded. 'And that's why I'm presenting it to you right now – to show you I'm serious about the truce.'

I glanced at Naomi. She was staring at the clover too, unsure of what to make of it.

'What?' I asked sternly. 'A truce? *Why?* Do you think I'm dumb?'

'No,' Wyatt answered straight-faced. 'I don't think you're dumb. In fact, I *know* you're more clever than I am, which is why you're here.'

'Get to the *point*,' Naomi demanded.

Wyatt grunted, staring at her, and then turned back to me. 'The gum theft has sparked my interest, and I'm asking for a truce so that the two of us can work together to find the... *bandit.* It's obvious that there's something fishy going on, and I'd like to get to the bottom of it. You know that Olive and I are together, and you know how much she loves her gum. I'd like to figure this out... to keep her from becoming a victim of the Buchanan bandit.' Wyatt paused. 'Clever, right? Buchanan bandit? I *just* thought of that. Like, right now.'

'You want our clans to team up?' I asked, dumbfounded.

Wyatt shook his head. 'No, not our clans. Just us. You and me. Two people.'

I didn't need to waste another second thinking about it. 'No way,' I said coldly. 'There's no way I can trust you. You've burned me too many times for that.'

Clenching his jaw, Wyatt spoke through his teeth. 'I believe this bandit situation is bigger than any of us know. Don't come running back to me when this whole thing blows up in your face.'

'Right. This whole thing is gonna blow up in my face,' I replied with as much sarcasm as I could muster. I turned my back on him and headed back to the cafeteria. Naomi followed, leaving Wyatt in the beat-up leather chair with his waffle cook.

'You'll be sorry,' Wyatt sneered as we walked away.

It took all my strength to look like I had it together, but the truth was that I didn't. With my history at Buchanan, the entire situation *could* blow up in my face, and that was a scary thought.

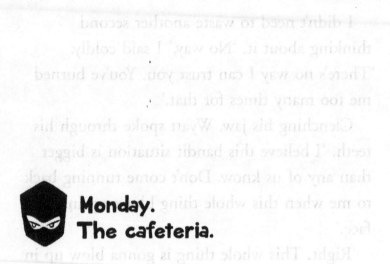

Monday.
The cafeteria.

Naomi playfully punched my arm and said I had made the right decision before heading back to her table. Deep down I knew that I had, but I still couldn't shake the feeling that I had made a mistake.

I took a seat on the edge of the stage, staring at nothing, going over every word of Wyatt's conversation in my head. Was Wyatt really offering a truce? And if he was, what then? Was I supposed to forget everything that's happened? Is that what adults mean when they say to forgive and forget?

The problem was that I still didn't fully trust him. Can you blame me? One afternoon and a Belgian waffle was supposed to make us BFFs?

'Something's wrong,' Zoe said.

I rubbed my eyes, bringing my head down from the clouds. 'Huh?' I grunted. 'What's the matter? What's wrong?'

'No,' Zoe said, letting out a breath of air through her nose. She took a spot next to me. Together, we watched the students in the cafeteria live their totally normal lives in a school they didn't realise *wasn't* so normal. 'I mean, something's wrong with *you*.'

Zoe could read me like a book – I guess that's what happens with cousins. I debated whether or not to tell her about Wyatt, but ultimately decided it was best if she didn't know… at least for now. 'Yeah, I mean, no,' I said. 'Nothing's wrong.'

'Chaaaaaase,' she sang. 'C'mon, don't be a baby. Just tell me what's going on.'

I took a second to respond. 'I was just thinking… Isn't life supposed to go back to normal after some kind of crazy event?'

'You mean how Wyatt became the vice president?' she asked.

'Sorta,' I said, tilting my head from side to side. 'I mean, once the day is saved, things should chill out, shouldn't they? We've saved the day quite a few times, and it doesn't ever seem to go back to the way things were. When Wyatt became the hall monitor captain, he *stayed* the hall monitor captain! And now he's *still* the vice president! Shouldn't he just go back to being a bully with no power?'

'Um, yeah,' Zoe said, raising an eyebrow. 'That's because this is real life and not a television show. The universe doesn't reset at the end of the day. You've watched too much TV. Things change – life *changes* – and you have to adapt.'

'You mean, like, the way a video game changes its difficulty setting if you're too good?'

Zoe stared at me for a moment. 'No,' she finally said. 'Not like that.'

I sighed, feeling like my body was sinking into itself.

'I think I'd go crazy if things went back to normal at the end of every day,' Zoe said.

'Why?' I asked, curious.

'It just sounds so *boring*, doesn't it? If life didn't move forward, then nothing could ever grow.'

'Ugh,' I groaned. 'Flowers?'

'No, dork,' Zoe said. '*Us.* I mean that *we* would never grow. We'd stay the same boring immature kids forever if we didn't go through a single challenge. If we didn't fail or make any mistakes, we wouldn't have to overcome them and we wouldn't grow up or get stronger.'

The bell for the end of school rang out over our conversation. Zoe bounced up and turned back to face me. 'You know what I mean?'

I slipped off the stage too. 'I think so,' I said.

Zoe smiled and then spun around and jogged over to Gavin. I joined the swarm of students walking toward the exit of the cafeteria.

Maybe Zoe was right. Maybe life shouldn't reset at the end of every episode. I wouldn't be who I was if it weren't for the crazy year I've had so far, right? Right then I decided that maybe siding with Wyatt was a good idea. And even if it wasn't, it'd be a mistake that I'd learn from.

Besides, it was possible that Wyatt had changed his ways. Wasn't it?

**Tuesday.
Before homeroom.**

When I got to school, I went straight for my locker. Digging through the pile of rubbish in my locker, I found the books for my morning classes and a pen that wasn't dried out. I slipped them into my book bag too.

I attached my name tag from the day before to one of my shoelaces. My plan was to find Wyatt to continue the conversation we had backstage yesterday. I felt a little uneasy about it, but I kept reminding myself that people *could* change.

As I zipped up my bag, I overheard some kids behind me talking.

'Did you hear that Jesse's gum got stolen?'

'No way! So did Matt and Rachel's! Right from their backpacks, which is weird because Rachel said she keeps her lunch money in the same pocket as her gum, but the money wasn't even touched!'

'I know, right? A friend of mine keeps his gum in a small pouch along with the rest of his lollies, but the thief only took the gum!'

There were conversations like that in every hallway. There was something crummy going on, that was for sure. It sounds like almost everyone in the school is a victim – it's a spree.

The Buchanan bandit must be pretty smart to *only* be taking gum. They probably know kids won't say anything because it's something they shouldn't even have.

But even as I walked to homeroom, I noticed that a bunch of kids were chewing on gum. At first I thought those students were the bandits until I realised the ones who were chomping were completely random kids, spread out down the hallway. None of them were part of the same groups, which could only mean they weren't victims ... *yet*.

Just then, I felt someone nudge my back. My stomach dropped because I thought it was going to be someone I didn't want to see. Thankfully, I was wrong.

'Sorry, man,' said another sixth grader. I recognised him, but I had never spoken to him before. He skulked back, keeping his hands cupped close to his chest.

'No problemo,' I said with a tight smile. In his hands was a pink eraser – actually *two* erasers. They were like the one that nailed my noggin the day before and they were so bright that they were impossible to miss. 'Cool erasers.'

The boy shot me a dirty look. 'Keep your grubby paws off them! They're mine!' he growled.

I was shocked. 'They're just erasers.'

'I said they're mine!' the boy shouted, licking the sides of both erasers. When he was done, he stared at me with raised eyebrows like he had just won an argument we never had.

'Alright, man,' I said, breaking eye contact. 'Whatever.'

'That's right,' he said as I walked away. 'They're *mine*.'

I didn't look back, but I could feel his eyes burning holes in the back of my head. 'Weirdo,' I whispered.

**Tuesday.
Homeroom.**

The bell rang just as I set foot in homeroom. I even dove into my seat before it *stopped* ringing. Ninja skills.

Zoe was in front of me and Brayden was at his usual spot on my left. His head was buried in his arms on the desk, the universal signal to leave someone alone because they were trying to catch a nap. It might be the universal signal for crying too. I don't know.

Mrs Robinson, our homeroom teacher, was playing with a brown paper bag on her desk while the rest of the students waited patiently.

Finally, she patted a stack of papers together, leaned back, and started the morning announcements.

'Good morning, students,' Mrs Robinson said loudly. 'Today is day two of careers week, and assuming everything goes as it should, your test results should be in and you ought to get paired with a mentor from your chosen field.'

'Not chosen by *us*,' I whispered sarcastically, leaning forward so Zoe could hear me.

She shrugged and kept her eyes on the front of the room.

Mrs Robinson continued. 'Like yesterday, classes will be as usual until after lunch, and then all sixth-grade students will meet in the cafeteria.' She paused, studying her sheet of notes, looking as though she was trying to make sense of something. 'I guess the mentors will already be at your table? It's not clear from this.'

Nobody seemed to mind.

Standing, Mrs Robinson picked up the brown paper bag. By the way she was gripping the bag, it obviously had something heavy inside.

'As an added bonus,' Mrs Robinson said, 'the school is giving every sixth grader an eraser.'

The room fell silent – the kind of silence that creeps you out in a movie theatre just before the monster jumps out. Everyone looked at each other, confused. But all of a sudden, kids exploded with cheers and shouts of joy.

Brayden jerked awake. He grabbed the sides of his desk and looked panicked. I laughed.

Mrs Robinson handed the kid in the first seat a stack of erasers. 'Take one and pass the rest on,' she said.

'What just happened?' Brayden asked, staring into space.

'A werewolf was just spotted north of here,' Zoe said with a straight face. 'A team of special forces has been dispatched and are hoping to capture the beast alive.'

Brayden blinked. 'Nuh-uh,' he said.

Zoe and I laughed.

'Seriously,' Brayden said. 'Nuh-uh, right?'

'What do *you* think?' Zoe asked.

Brayden fell silent.

'Oh my god,' Zoe said, shaking her head and smiling. '*No*, they didn't find a werewolf, alright? I was joking.'

Brayden pressed his lips together as he rubbed his forehead. 'Don't even *joke* about that,' he said. 'So why'd everyone freak out just now?'

Zoe turned in her chair. 'Everyone's getting an eraser.'

'No,' Brayden said. 'I mean, why did everyone shout like that?'

Zoe raised her eyebrows at him. 'Because *everyone's getting an eraser*.'

'Oh,' Brayden replied. 'Cool...I guess.'

'Yeah, what's the deal with those things?' I asked. 'I saw a kid before with a couple of them. He kinda freaked when I mentioned them. And then he...*licked* 'em.'

'Sick.' Zoe smirked as she took two erasers from the student in front of her. She turned back and joked, 'They're what's *hot* in the *streets*. Haven't you heard? You ain't cool unless you got one of these.'

'But they're just erasers,' I said, taking one from Zoe's hand. 'Who cares?'

Brayden smiled as he studied his eraser. 'You collect comics, right?'

'Right,' I replied.

'Well, think of these erasers like that,' Brayden said. 'Remember a few years ago when everyone was collecting those rubber-band bracelets shaped like random things?'

I smiled, tilting my head slowly like I was remembering a fond memory. 'Yeaaaaaah. Those dinosaur ones were *bananas.*'

Zoe laughed. 'Dork.'

'Still though,' I said, staring at the pink block in my hand, 'I just don't see the appeal in these things.'

Before Brayden or Zoe could reply, the bell rang. Everyone in class pulled their book bags over their shoulders and poured out of the room.

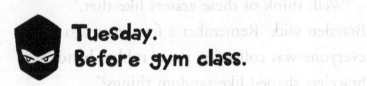

Tuesday.
Before gym class.

I always took the east hallway to gym class. The gymnasium was in that direction, but Faith also has a class over there. Talking to her was always a good way to kill time before class.

When I found her, Gavin was standing with her.

'Sup, noob?' Faith said, leaning against the lockers outside her classroom.

'The sky,' I said, regretting it immediately. My brain screamed, *Why do you keep trying to make that funny? It's not funny! It's never been funny, and it never* will *be funny! As punishment, here's some forehead sweat.*

And yeah, my forehead started to sweat.

Faith laughed anyway.

'Nice,' Gavin said.

Changing the subject, I pointed at Gavin. 'Actually I was hoping to see you. I still think we should try and figure out who's been stealing the gum.'

Gavin was quick to respond. 'Nuh-uh, no sir. I told ya yesterday, I can't be a part of all that this time. Zoe made a pretty good point in saying we shouldn't get involved. Remember what happened last time? We found a secret ninja hideout fulla red ninjas.'

'Seriously?' Faith asked, intrigued. 'You did?'

I shut my eyes and sighed. '*Maybe.*'

'This just seems like more trouble than it's worth,' Gavin said. 'You know what sounds good to me? Having a normal school day. The kind of day where ya get to school hoping to catch some rest and relaxation, zoning in and out until the last bell. *That* sounds like an excellent day.'

I was disappointed to hear Gavin say that. Out of all my friends, I thought for sure *he'd* be the one who would want to seek justice.

'But something is going on!' I said. 'Isn't it weird that a ton of gum is being stolen, and *only* gum?'

Gavin paused. '*Only* gum, huh?'

Gavin was interested – I could tell by the twinkle in his eye.

Shaking his head, Gavin glanced at his wristwatch. 'No, I can't. I'm sorry, but I just can't.'

'Bummer,' Faith said as Gavin walked away.

'I know, right?' I said.

Faith fell silent for a second, and then she said softly, 'My gum was stolen this morning too.'

My heart sunk. 'No way! Why didn't you say anything?'

'I'm saying something now,' Faith replied. 'It was in my pocket and everything.'

'They managed to get it from your *pocket*?'

Faith nodded. 'During the break between homeroom and first period. I had it when I left homeroom, and when I got to first period, it was gone.'

'Did anything happen to you during the break? Anyone bump into you?'

Faith twisted her lips to one side of her face. 'Nope, nothing. Nobody bumped into me. Nobody even talked to me.'

This was serious. This wasn't just a bandit, it was a *skilled* bandit…maybe even a *ninja* bandit. It was already a big deal, but now that the bandit had stolen from a friend, it was personal.

'Maybe he's right though,' Faith said, pointing in the direction that Gavin had walked. 'Maybe this case isn't worth investigating. I'm not even mad. It was a dollar pack of gum.'

'It might be just a cheap pack of gum,' I said, 'but that's *not* the point. The point is that someone thinks it's okay to steal other people's stuff. Something has to be done. All it takes for bad guys to win is for the good guys to do nothing, and I don't want to be the guy that just stood by and did nothing.'

'You know what else is considered 'doing something'?' Faith asked.

I shook my head, but I knew what she was going to say.

'Telling the principal,' she said.

'But he *won't* do anything,' I said defensively. '*None* of the teachers will because nobody's supposed to have gum anyway.'

Faith shrugged but didn't say anything else.

The bell rang loudly. Faith smiled and gave me a quick hug, telling me not to do anything stupid. I promised her I'd try my best.

I was already late for gym, but everyone showed up late anyway. Coach Cooper never really cared.

This Buchanan bandit situation was starting to look more like an epic disaster than petty theft. It might seem like a silly thing to worry about because, like Faith said, it's just a pack of gum, and while just a pack of gum might be a lame-sounding crime, it gets a lot worse when it becomes a *boatload* of gum.

I wonder what a boatload of gum would even look like.

**Tuesday.
The locker room.**

The locker room was pretty empty by the time
I made it there. Coach Cooper was sitting at
the computer in his office, playing that card
game everyone plays. I can never remember
what it's called, but when you beat it, the cards
bounce all over the screen. *Thrilling*, right?

I walked down the aisle to my locker. I was
deep in thought, holding my book bag straps
tight around my shoulders.

During the first week of school, Wyatt was
in the same gym class as I was. When he came
back after his suspension, they put him in

another class. How strange that I was actually *wishing* we were in the same class again. It would make finding him much easier.

I craned my neck to the side, cracking it as my book bag hit the floor. The thump echoed off the green lockers in the empty room.

Coach Cooper had closed his computer game, and hadn't noticed that I was still in the room. He always stayed until the last kid left, probably to make sure nobody got into anything they shouldn't. Oh well. At least it was quiet.

I spun the dial on my locker and entered my combination. Gripping the metal latch, I was about to pull up until something caught my eye. I froze.

Someone had taped a note to the top of my locker.

It wasn't the first time someone left me a note, and it probably wouldn't be the last time either.

I glanced over my shoulder making sure I actually *was* alone. I snatched the slip of paper off the locker and unfolded it.

Keep your nose outta our business or else.

I chuckled loudly, in case the person who left the note was still in the room. I didn't want to show any sign that I was afraid or intimidated. I even spoke out loud. 'Pssssh! Or else *what?*'

The answer came when I opened the metal door of my gym locker. My jaw dropped as I stared at the wall of stolen gum packages that had been crammed so tightly into the small space that they didn't even fall out. They were like tiny bricks that stunk of spearmint.

'So *that's* what a boatload of gum looks like,' I whispered.

I slammed the door shut. The sound of metal against metal clanged across the locker room. Luckily there wasn't anyone in there.

'What's your problem?' a voice said from behind me.

At least I *thought* there wasn't anyone in there.

I set my hand on the cold metal surface of my locker. 'Heh, nothing,' I said in an embarrassingly high pitched voice. 'Sorry 'bout that. Sometimes I don't know my own strength!'

The boy glared at me. Finally, he rolled his eyes. 'Whatever,' he said before leaving the locker room.

My heart was pounding inside my chest, and for some reason I couldn't catch my breath. There I was, alone in the boys' locker room, with a locker full of stolen gum. I wish I could say it was a situation that was new to me, but it's really not.

Things had escalated way too quickly. First it was a pack of stolen gum, then it was *many*

packs of stolen gum, and now someone's zeroed
in on *me* specifically.

Why do these things always happen to me?

I sat, defeated, on the bench in the middle
of the aisle. I felt something underneath me.
When I slid over, I saw a red wristband. The
same red wristband that Wyatt's red ninjas
always wore.

RED NINJA BRACELET

I picked it up, thinking that maybe one of the red ninjas was behind the stolen gum, but then realised it was pretty unlikely. If a red ninja had planted the gum in my locker, then there was *no way* they'd be foolish enough to forget their wristband at the scene of the crime.

Another possibility was that whoever was trying to frame me was *also* trying to frame the red ninja clan. It was like they thought, *Oh, I'll just leave this red wristband here. That way Chase will believe the red ninjas did it!*

Too bad for them, I'm not as dumb as I am...

I mean, as dumb as I *think* I am...

No wait, as dumb as *they* think I am.

Never mind.

That was another reason for me to seek Wyatt's help, but I didn't want to wait until after lunch to find him. I needed to get hold of that kid asap, and I'm pretty sure I knew where to find him.

Tuesday.
Outside the red ninja hideout.

Coach Cooper excused me from class without
flinching. And I didn't even try to hide the
truth! I said there was a situation that needed
to be dealt with concerning some stolen
property, and that I wanted to find Wyatt to
talk about it. The coach waved his hand and
wished me luck.

Weird, right?

It took me a few minutes to get backstage in
the cafeteria. The first time I stumbled upon
the red ninjas hideout was when I was chasing
after the missing penguin last week. The bird

had escaped through a secret passage in the hall that led to an abandoned greenhouse where the red ninjas were training.

If you would've told me last week that I'd willingly walk back into their hideout, I would've laughed until tears streamed down my cheeks.

The only thought going through my head was, *What am I doing? What am I doing? What am I doing?*

Finally, I made it to the opening of the greenhouse. I could hear thumps and hollers as they trained together. It sounded a lot like I was standing outside a dance club. Leaning against the wall, I reconsidered what it was I was doing. Listening to the sound of the red ninjas training didn't help me feel better.

On the floor next to the opening were red ninja robes, folded nicely and stacked on top each other. I had to hand it to them – they were an organised, tidy bunch of kids. I don't even fold my clothes at home!

I stretched my arms out behind my back,

whispering to myself. 'Am I really gonna do this? Am I really gonna put on a red ninja outfit?'

Staring at the folded robes on the floor, I sighed. 'Yep, I sure am.'

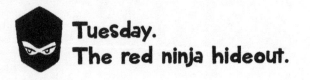

Tuesday.
The red ninja hideout.

I quickly slipped into the red robes. Wyatt had designed them to go right over street clothes. It was pretty smart actually, and I was a little jealous that I hadn't thought of it first. I took the red bracelet out of my pocket and held it tightly in my hand.

Without a second thought, I forced myself to enter the greenhouse.

The smell of dead plants lingered in the air, along with the scent of kids getting their sweat on by training. It was more musty than stinky.

As I passed other ninjas, they glanced at me,

nodding in greeting. I punched my open palm
and nodded back at them.

I could see Wyatt sitting in his leather chair
at the front of the greenhouse. He wasn't
wearing *any* of his ninja gear, which wasn't too
surprising. As the VP, he probably didn't want
to risk getting caught wearing it. With an
intense stare, he studied his ninjas as they threw
punches and kicks into the air.

Weaving through the crowd of red ninjas, I
made my way to the front of the room, hoping

nobody would recognise me since I was fully decked out in red ninja—

'Hey!' shouted one of the bigger red ninjas. He stepped in front of me, blocking my path to Wyatt.

'Not good,' I whispered.

'What do you think you're doing?' the ninja growled with a more feminine voice than I had originally heard. It was a girl under the mask. She was holding her fist out at me.

I wasn't sure how to respond, so I didn't say anything. By this time, everyone in the room was staring at me, *including* Wyatt.

'I said, *what* do you think you're doing?' she repeated.

A billion different emotions shot through my body. If I ran, I *might* be able to make it out of the room before they started chasing after me.

It was a personal decision I made long ago to never throw a punch, but I wasn't sure any of the ninjas surrounding me made the same decision. I was as good as dead.

The tall ninja pointed at the bracelet that

was in my death grip. 'You *wear* that thing with *pride*. It goes on your wrist, dummy!' she joked, laughing heartily.

The other ninjas in the greenhouse laughed with her.

The room started spinning as I gasped for air. Apparently my brain put my lungs on pause – it does dumb things like that sometimes. I tried laughing too, covering up the fact that I was actually catching my breath, as I pulled the bracelet over my wrist. I only hoped they couldn't see how badly my hands were shaking.

'I'm just messin' witchya,' the girl said before walking off.

I swallowed hard, looking back at Wyatt, still in his leather chair. Casually, I walked to the front of the room and stood by his side.

Wyatt didn't move a muscle. His head was resting in one hand as he watched the red ninjas train in the room. He almost looked bored.

Struggling with what to say, I leaned closer to him, but he spoke before I did.

WYATT'S CHAIR

ME (DECKED OUT IN RED NINJA GEAR)

WYATT

'Great day for training,' the leader of the red ninja clan said. 'Isn't that right, Chase?'

My jaw tightened, and I felt like I couldn't move again. At last, I asked, 'How'd you know?'

Wyatt spun his chair around to face me. 'You don't move the way my red ninjas move. You've got a different way about you.'

I wasn't sure whether to be proud of that fact or not.

Wyatt pointed at my shoes. 'Plus you're wearing a piece of paper with your name on it.'

I looked down at the name tag I had clipped to my shoe that morning. 'Stupid,' I whispered, scolding myself.

'Don't sweat it,' Wyatt said, chuckling. 'But you'd better get talkin' before anyone else in here figures out who you are. I'd tell them to leave you alone, but in a group this big, they might not hear me over the sound of their own anger.'

I took his advice, and began explaining myself right away. I told him about how the gum bandit was taking more than anyone realised, and how they're only focused on gum instead of other things that actually have *value*.

'And my friends have decided to sit this one out,' I said, 'but I didn't want to investigate alone... so that's why I'm here – to see if your offer still stands.'

'My offer to help?' Wyatt asked.

I nodded. The rest of the red ninjas in the room continued training without a clue about what was happening at the front of the greenhouse.

'Admit that you were wrong,' Wyatt demanded.

I was silent.

He smirked the same way I'd imagine an evil overlord would right before claiming victory over the world. 'Tell me I was right.'

Not wanting to waste any more time, I clenched my jaw. 'Fine. You *weren't* wrong.'

Wyatt paused, studying me with his narrow eyes. 'Good enough!'

'So that's that then?' I asked. 'Just like that we're working together?'

Wyatt spun again in his chair, grabbing a small box from the ground. 'Not quite,' he said. 'You burned me yesterday when you refused my offer first. I even went through the trouble of finding a four-leaf clover to show how serious I was.'

'Okaaaaay,' I said, suspicious. 'So?'

Wyatt's face grew angry, but he kept his voice down. 'So now *you* have to do something for me to prove that *you're* serious.'

'You want a four-leaf clover? I'll get you a four-leaf clover,' I said, even though it was Zoe

74

that found the clover back at the beginning of the year.

'No,' Wyatt said, tapping the cardboard box in his lap. 'All you have to do is take this to the principal's office.'

'Yeah?' I asked. 'That's all I have to do, huh? Is that box filled with money or something?'

That was part of my first week at Buchanan too. Taking a bag full of money to the principal's office to frame Zoe for theft.

Wyatt peeled open the top of the box. He held out a handful of erasers – the ones that everyone was going nuts over, but not just pink ones. 'I promise that the box only has these dumb little things in it.'

'What's the deal with these anyway?' I asked, suddenly aware of a nasty spearmint scent in the air. I glanced at the red ninjas in the room and wondered which one of them was Olive.

'These little erasers are Sebastian's own creation,' Wyatt explained. 'He created these to coincide with the careers week stuff. It's all about sales and marketing and blah blah blah, y'know?'

'So he's the one handing these things out?'

'He's *selling* them,' Wyatt said.

'How's he allowed to do that?' I asked.

Wyatt sighed. 'For every eraser sold, he donates ten cents to the school. Since they're selling so well, the school is considering selling them through the supply shop for a buck a pop.'

'A dollar?' I said loudly. 'He's making *ninety cents* off these things? But my homeroom teacher handed out a ton of these for *free* this morning!'

Wyatt laughed. 'That's right. The school *bought* all those erasers from Sebastian so they could do that. I guess Principal Davis is all for the idea of Sebastian starting a business, especially since it's careers week. There's probably a great lesson to be learned about money and economics, but... whatever, I don't care.'

I took one of the erasers and looked at it. It was bright blue and had a thin piece of card wrapped around it. Sebastian's picture and logo

76

were also on the paper. 'I've gotta hand it to the kid – he knows how to sell a product.'

'Right?' Wyatt said as he shoved the box into my hands. 'So get this to the principal's office. There's nothing shady about my request. They know the box is coming, but I'm just too lazy to take it there myself,' he said smiling, and holding his hand out for me to shake it.

Without hesitating, I grabbed my enemy's hand and shook it like a businessman.

I nodded at a few of the red ninjas on my way out. They still didn't have a clue who I was.

Once I was clear of the greenhouse, I took off the red ninja robes, dumping them in one of the drama club boxes backstage. With the box of erasers in my arms, I headed straight for the front office.

Tuesday.
The front office.

When I walked into the air-conditioned front office, a young woman with blonde hair tied back in a ponytail greeted me. I'd never seen her before, so she probably wasn't a teacher.

'Can I help you?' she asked, standing at the counter and chewing the end of her pencil.

I set the box of erasers on the counter and flipped open the lid. 'I'm supposed to drop these off here?'

The woman's smile was bright enough to light up a dark room. '*Fantastic!* We've been

78

waiting all morning for these! Principal Davis
will be thrilled.'

'Coooooooool,' I said suavely. 'So I'll just
leave them with you, and that's it?'

'That's it,' the woman replied sliding the box
off the other side of the front counter. 'Just tell
me your name so I can let Principal Davis know
who delivered them. I know he'll want to know
how helpful you were.'

With a smile beaming across my face, I said,
'Chase Cooper.'

'Thanks, Chase,' the woman said.

I turned around just in time to hear the lunch bell. Before the front lobby was completely swarming with students, I managed to make it across the hall so I could stand in front of the tinted windows of the cafeteria and wait for my friends.

'Over here!' Faith shouted in front of the lunchroom doors.

Brayden and Gavin stood behind her, waiting in the lunch line. Zoe wasn't around, which meant that she was probably in the library with the other zombies.

Yes, zombies.

The smartest kids in school, aka 'smarties', were allowed to sit in the library during lunch so they could have an extra study period during the day. It was *meant* to be a reward so they could spend the time doing extra research for any classes or projects. It was the only time during the day when surfing the internet on your phone was allowed. I guess the school hoped the smarties would appreciate the responsibility and use their time wisely.

In reality, pretty much all the smarties spent the entire time staring at their phones, texting friends and sharing dumb videos of cute animals doing silly things. Have you ever seen kids hypnotised by a smart-phone screen? They look like zombies.

Zoe claims she actually uses that time for research, but I know better. She's just as zombified as the rest of them when she's in there.

A short while back, I found myself in the midst of the library zombies, and trust me, it's a lot scarier than it sounds. After that fateful day, I vowed never to return to the land of the library zombies.

I walked over to Faith, Gavin and Brayden, and we went into the lunchroom together to eat whatever terrible item was on the menu for the day.

**Tuesday.
The careers fair.**

Right after lunch was over, I went straight for my careers week table. Dozens of mentors were already circling the room, talking with the students they had been paired with, and I couldn't wait to see what my career results were.

Waiting patiently in my seat, I strained my eyes to see what careers my friends had got. It almost felt like Christmas morning, but without the presents, and without it being December, and without the eggnog, pecan pie, or spiced tea. Okay, so it was *nothing* like Christmas morning. It didn't matter how hard I looked for my friends though because there were too many people in the room to see anything past three metres in front of me anyway.

I spun in my chair and opened the manila folder in front of me. My mentor was running a few minutes late, but maybe there was some information in the packet about what my career was.

Sure enough, I found a new slip of paper that had my test results on it!

All I had to do was skim the page and find out what kind of amazing life my future held. Video game designer? Comic book artist? Astronaut? Was it *at all* possible that my test paired me with a *ninja*?

Oh man! What if it *did*? I've been wondering why my mentor wasn't there yet, but...what if he was? What if it was a ninja so good at ninja-ing that he was completely invisible somewhere out in the open?

My eyes skimmed faster down the page until I finally found what I was looking for.

There it was – my name, Chase Cooper, with

a bunch of dashes that trailed to the other side of the page, connecting with the career that I—

Chase Cooper––––––––––––*Circus Clown*

'Wait, *what*?'

Honka honka honka honka!

The paper fell from my hands. I watched it float past my black sneakers and across the floor, landing in front of a pair of humongous red shoes.

'Hey there, kiddo!' a man wearing a full face of make-up said. 'We're gonna have a *honkin'* fun time!'

His face became emotionless as he stared at me, honking his stinkin' clown horn like his life depended on it.

Honka honka honka honka honka honka honka honka honka honka honka honka honka honka honka honka honka honka honka!

I kid you not, every single person in the room stopped what they were doing to see the source of the most annoying sound in the world.

'*Stop that!*' I hissed. '*You're embarrassing me!*'

The clown tap danced his oversized shoes towards me, which was frightening by itself, but tap dancing apparently wasn't enough. No, this clown also wanted to start blowing up one of those long balloons they make balloon animals out of.

So yeah, this *monster* was staring into my soul while twisting a long balloon into an animal and *also* tap dancing straight at me, and in a roomful of spectators. The silence only made the squeaking balloons and taps that much worse.

I'm not gonna lie. I feared for my life.

'Okay, I was wrong,' I whispered. '*This* is how I die…'

The clown did his tap-dance finale in front of me and extended an open hand. 'The name's Miko! My friends call me Miko, but *you* can call me *Miko!*'

I slouched in my seat. 'My name's Chase,' I said. 'You can call me Chase.'

'Pleasure to make your acquaintance, Chase!'

Miko said gleefully, with his hand still outstretched towards me.

I made a fist and bumped his open palm with it. He dropped his hand and took a seat next to me.

'Just my luck,' I groaned. 'I get paired with a freak show.'

Miko wagged his finger at me. 'Now *that's* not vewy nice,' he said in a goofy voice.

MIKO

TINY HAT

FLOWER THAT PROB'LY SQUIRTS WATER.

MIGHT BE HIS REAL HAIR

EMPTY EYES

SUSPENDERS PLUS BELT?? Can we say redundant?

ANNOYING HORN!

OVERSIZED NECKTIE

FINAL VERDICT? GROSS!

I shook my head, rubbing my eyes. 'No, you're right. I'm sorry. I was just expecting something...different.'

'Everyone does,' Miko said, his silly voice slightly trailing away.

I leaned back, trying to make the best of the situation. 'So like, this is your career then? Like, your job is to dress like a clown and stuff?'

'Yep,' Miko said, honking his horn once. *Honka!*

'Please stop,' I said flatly. 'So like, why? Why be a clown? Did you drop out of university or something?'

'Actually,' Miko said, using his real voice, which was much deeper than I expected. 'I had to go to university to do this.'

I blinked. 'What?'

'Yep,' Miko continued. 'I went to theatre school and chose to be a clown. I guess I'm just one of those guys who never really grew up, y'know? I just grew older.'

I blinked, only half listening to what the

clown was saying. I was too busy imagining a real ninja hiding somewhere in the cafeteria.

'Don't you regret it?' I asked.

Miko stared at me for a moment. 'As a matter of fact, *no*, I *don't* regret it. I gotta say,' he wagged his finger at me again, 'you're a bit insensitive, aren't you?'

I was silent, unsure what to say and a little embarrassed.

The clown continued. 'Hey, man. I'm just dishin' out the same stuff you're cookin', am I right?' He started honking his insanely loud horn at my face again. *Honka honka honka honka!*

I stood up and started walking away, but Miko jumped up too. He tossed the balloon animal in the air and started patting it upwards with both hands. And then, as loudly as possible, he said, '*Hey, Chase! Don't let the balloon touch the ground! Woo hoo!*'

I didn't know if anyone was even paying attention, but I'd never been more embarrassed in my life. 'Just leave me alone, okay? Go back to the table.'

Miko let the balloon drift to the ground. 'Whatever you say, boss. I get paid to be here whether I'm mentoring or not.' He turned and sat back down.

I scurried across the room, feeling mortified that Miko had made such a scene. I just wanted to find my friends in the crowded cafeteria so I could relax a little with them.

I heard Zoe's voice through the crowd. 'So *what's* his job?'

When I made it to their table, I saw what my friends were talking about. Brayden was sitting next to some guy wearing a giant wolf costume. At least I wasn't the only one who got a strange career mentor.

'Wearing a wolf costume,' Brayden answered.

'How'd you manage to get that?' Faith asked. 'What'd you say on your test?'

Brayden paused. 'I was trying to manipulate the test so I'd get paired with a werewolf *hunter*...'

'But instead you got a guy in a wolf costume?' Zoe asked. *'How's that even a career?'*

'Hey!' the guy in the costume snipped. 'I didn't choose to wear this wolf costume; it chose *me*!'

'Could be worse, dude,' I said. 'At least you didn't get a *clown*.'

I glanced over my shoulder at Miko, who was still wearing that creepy grin. A chill ran down my spine.

Gavin was sitting with his mentor, who looked like he was dressed for something sporty.

'I'm not saying ya shouldn't be here, I'm just sayin' that maybe there was a mistake with my test! I was expectin' to get some sort of soil job,' Gavin said. 'Y'see, my daddy was a soil man, just like *his* daddy before that, and his *daddy's* daddy before that! I come from a long line of soil men ... Men proud of soilin' themselves.'

'There's gotta be a better way of saying that,' Zoe groaned.

'Sorry, dude,' Gavin's mentor said. 'Your test results don't lie. You got stuck with a rock climber.'

'You mean you rock climb professionally?' Gavin asked.

Gavin's mentor nodded. 'Yessir. Been doin' it since I was a tiny kid.'

'I didn't even know that rock climbing was a career,' I said.

The man gave me a half smile. 'Technically, it's not. I mean, there are some people out there *killin'* it with their climbing skills, and those are the guys who are sponsored by soft drink companies and stuff. *Those* guys can call it a career.'

On the table in front of him were a few of his climbing tools. There were bundles of rope and a bunch of carabiners. You know, those metal things that keep rock climbers from falling off the side of a mountain (or thing that hipsters use as a keychain).

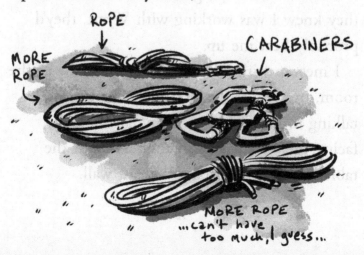

MORE
ROPE

ROPE

CARABINERS

MORE ROPE
...can't have
too much, I guess...

'So you wouldn't say rock climbing is your job?' Gavin asked, confused.

The man leaned forward with a *serious* look and stared deep into Gavin's eyes. 'Rock climbing is a way of *life*, brother. It's my reason for living. It's the *blood* in my veins.'

Gavin didn't even try to argue. 'Okay then, I guess I can respect that.'

From the corner of my eye, I saw Wyatt, but I knew it was because he *wanted* me to see him.

'I'll be right back, guys,' I said taking a few steps away.

Faith stood up. 'Wait, where are you going?'

'I, uh, have to go to the bathroom!' I said. 'Okay? BRB!'

I didn't like keeping secrets from them, but if they knew I was working with Wyatt, they'd probably beat me up.

I met up with Wyatt on the other side of the room, but had to make it look like I *wasn't* talking to him. He was sitting at one table, facing the west wall, so I took a seat at the table behind him, facing the east wall.

Naomi plopped herself down in the chair across from me. 'What do you think you're doing?' she asked.

I scanned the room to see if anyone had noticed us.

'Nothing, alright?' I said. 'I got this under control.'

'Yeah,' Wyatt said from behind me, still facing the opposite direction. 'Beat it, will ya?'

Naomi leaned over and stared past me. '*Really?* You're doing this?'

'We're not doing anything wrong,' I said. 'Wyatt's helping me catch the bandit.'

Naomi shook her head. 'Nuh-uh, not alone.'

'C'mon, Naomi,' I pleaded. 'This isn't something you want to get mixed up in.'

'But you do?' she retorted.

I nodded. 'Seriously, we can take care of it ourselves.'

Naomi folded her hands and looked at me like I was a child. 'I'm not going anywhere. You two are going to play nicely, and *I'm* going to make sure of it.'

Wyatt shook his head, growling in frustration. 'Fine! Whatever! Just keep out of our way, and you can tag along, alright?'

'Deal,' Naomi said with satisfied smile.

Just then Sebastian entered the cafeteria with Principal Davis trailing behind him. Sebastian gestured as he spoke to the principal, pointing toward the back corner of the cafeteria. Principal Davis laughed at something and nodded his head.

'What's that all about?' I asked.

Wyatt peeked over his shoulder. 'Oh, remember how I said Principal Davis *loves* the fact that Sebastian has created a mini business during careers week?'

'Yeah,' I said.

'Well, he loves it so much that he's letting Sebastian sell them in the Pit,' Wyatt said. 'They hope to have the Pit fully stocked by Friday.'

'No way,' Naomi said. 'Good for Sebastian, I guess. He seems to be a really successful kid, doesn't he?'

'He just knows the right people,' Wyatt said. 'In this school, it's all about who you know.'

'So Sebastian made those little erasers?' Naomi asked. 'Heads are exploding over those things.'

Wyatt sighed. 'Listen, we don't have much time, and it's going to start looking strange if anyone sees us talking to ourselves so let's make this quick, shall we?'

'What's the plan?' I asked.

'Tomorrow morning,' Wyatt said. 'Be here at 7:30 sharp, and bring a pack of gum.'

'*7:30?*' I said. 'But I don't even wake up until 8:30!'

'What?' Naomi said. 'That gives you less than twenty minutes to get dressed and get to school on time.'

'Correct,' I said, pointing finger guns at her.

Naomi frowned. 'Your parents must hate you in the morning.'

'Correct again!' I said, pointing my finger guns again. I turned my head slightly so Wyatt could hear me. 'Is there a little wiggle room in this schedule of yours? Like, maybe we can just meet after homeroom or something?'

Wyatt didn't answer.

When I looked over my shoulder, he wasn't there anymore. 'Did you see him leave?' I asked Naomi.

She shook her head. 'Say whatever you want about that kid, but he's got serious ninja skills.'

My gut twisted. The way Wyatt was able to disappear like that made me uncomfortable, and I hoped that teaming up with him wasn't the biggest mistake of my life.

Naomi looked over her shoulder, watching

Sebastian across the room. 'Do you think the rumours are true?'

I had no idea what she was talking about. 'Huh?' I grunted like an ape. 'What rumours?'

'Y'know,' she said, lowering her voice. 'The rumours about the *Scavengers*. Do you think there's any truth to their existence?'

I leaned back, confused. 'What are you talking about?'

Naomi looked at me, slightly surprised. 'You haven't heard about them? How long have you been at this school?'

I ignored her question. 'Isn't a scavenger, like, an animal that feeds on things that are already dead?'

Naomi nodded and kept looking over both her shoulders like she was paranoid someone was there. 'Yeah,' she said. 'But they're also people who collect stuff that others throw away.'

I was beginning to feel a bit paranoid too. 'What do you mean? Is there a group of kids around here like that?'

Naomi shrugged her shoulders. 'Nobody

knows for sure,' she said. 'But nobody ever talks about it either.'

'Why not?'

Naomi paused. 'Because the rumour is that the Scavengers are the ones who really control what's going on at Buchanan. They're the ones in charge. Supposedly Sebastian is one of them, but it's never been proven.'

'Does everyone know about this rumour?' I asked.

'No,' Naomi said. 'But I figured that maybe you'd have at least heard about it since, y'know, you're the leader of a secret ninja clan.'

Great. As if the red ninja clan wasn't enough for me to worry about, now I've got another secret club that's apparently *so secret* almost nobody even knows that they even exist. If this was how sixth grade was, I didn't even want to *think* about what horrors seventh grade possibly held.

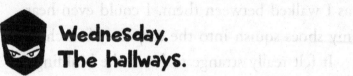

Wednesday.
The hallways.

I got my mum to drop me off a few minutes before Wyatt wanted me to meet him. This meant waking up at the butt-crack of dawn when the sun has barely risen. You ever wake up before the sun has? It's really weird.

Once I was in the school lobby, I took a left and started down the hall. Principal Davis was already in his office typing away on his computer. Most of the other office staff were doing the same.

The school was so quiet that I could hear the basketball team practising in the gym.

The sound of squeaking tennis shoes and balls echoed in the hallways.

There was something pleasant about how quiet and empty the corridors were. I think my dad would have called it *tranquil* – it means peaceful. Metal lockers loomed silently over me as I walked between them. I could even hear my shoes squish into the carpet with each step.

It felt really strange to be in the building before anyone else was. I felt ... *free*. Whenever I walk these halls, I always make sure I don't accidentally bump into someone, or I have to walk at a turtle's pace because a group of kids are staring at their phones and texting each other. But this morning, I could run as fast as I wanted without having to worry about anyone else.

And that's exactly what I did.

I clutched my book bag straps tighter and took off like a fox. Cold air streamed past my ears as I pushed myself harder to make it to the end of the corridor. The lockers on both sides of me became a blur, and for a second I imagined myself travelling back in time to when I first started at Buchanan.

I remember the first time I stepped into the humongous lobby out front, and the sense of fear and excitement that came over me. I didn't recognise a single person in the crowd that day. I wonder if Faith or Brayden were there too, and if they were, did they notice the new kid?

The end of the hall was coming up fast, but it connected with another hallway that I could easily turn into. I figure a couple of laps would probably be a good way to jolt my system awake, so instead of slowing down, I sped up.

Big mistake.

Just as I turned the corner, I felt a sharp pain in my knees. The floor disappeared from underneath me and the entire hallway flipped upside-down as I slammed into the wall. Maybe zooming around corners without looking both ways was a bad idea.

There was a sound like a cardboard box hitting the ground, and then several colourful little bricks bounced around me.

'What's the *matter* with you?' an angry boy shouted at me, holding one of his shins. 'You almost busted my leg!'

I sat up and leaned against the wall. 'Sorry about that,' I said as I rubbed my eyes.

The little bricks around me were Sebastian's erasers. There were tons of them were scattered down the hall.

'Really, I'm—' I stopped when I realised who was on the floor next to me.

It was Jake, leader of the wolf pack.

Oh yeah, and he's also a member of Wyatt's red ninja clan. I could see the red wristband.

I didn't want any trouble, so I scooped up a few of the erasers and held them out to Jake. He batted my hand away, knocking the erasers out of it. 'Keep your meat hooks off of those! You want one, you can buy it from the Pit!'

I was surprised. 'So they're letting him sell these through the Pit for sure?' I asked.

Jake rolled his eyes at me as he tossed the tiny coloured bricks back into the box. 'Uh duh, why else would I tell you to buy one there? Try using your brain sometime, it really helps conversations move forward rather than in circles.'

I stayed quiet. If I kept talking, it was only going to make things worse. I'd probably toss an insult, and then he'd toss one back, and it would keep going like that until he snapped and came at me like a banshee. Sometimes it is better to say nothing.

Jake dumped the rest of the erasers back into the box and hoisted it into his arms. With one last dirty look, he continued towards the lobby.

Sebastian must have been making a fortune with those erasers, especially if he's got a few people working for him. First it was Wyatt who needed to deliver a box of erasers to the front office, and now Jake was doing a delivery.

I felt a cold breeze on my back and heard the side door to the school seal itself shut.

Naomi's voice came from behind me. 'Good morning.'

I turned and saw her walking toward me, both hands pushed into the front pouch of her hoodie. 'Whassup,' I said.

'Seen Wyatt anywhere yet?' Naomi asked, peeking down the hall.

I shook my head. 'Nuh-uh, but he also didn't say where to meet him. He just kinda *vanished*.'

'Or maybe I've been here the entire time,' came an eerie voice from one of the classrooms in the hall. The door was open about a crack, and there was an eyeball pressed against the opening.

'Do you live here?' Naomi asked sarcastically.

The door swung open and Wyatt stepped into the hallway. 'Maybe,' he said, grinning. 'Maybe not. The key to being a good ninja is being mysterious.'

Naomi curled her lip. 'How long have you been hiding in that classroom? Minutes? Hours? Did you sneak in there when you saw me and Chase talking? That means you had to sneak into the room from the other side and then tiptoe in the darkness until you made it to the door, which *also* means you had to silently unlock it so we wouldn't hear it, *all* so you could be creepy and say, '*Maybe I've been here the whole time.*' Dude, seriously? If you're doing *all* that just so you can look cool, then you need to re-evaluate how you spend your time.'

Wyatt's grin faded. 'Maybe,' he hissed, probably because he couldn't think of a good comeback. 'Maybe not.'

Naomi stuck her tongue out, scrunching her face to mock him. '*Maybe. Maybe not,*' she said in a little kid's voice.

Wyatt took a step toward her, but I stood between them.

'Can we just get to the part about catching the bandit? We're wasting time.'

The muscles in Wyatt's jaw twitched. 'Agreed,' he said. 'Did you bring a pack of gum?'

I pulled out a rectangular pack of cinnamon gum from my pocket. My mum let me take one of her packs – she's got a million of them in a junk drawer that *reeks* of cinnamon.

'Excellent,' Wyatt wheezed as he tapped his fingers together. 'We're going to set a trap for the bandit this morning and use your gum as bait.'

I was confused but curious. 'Like, we're gonna tie a string to it or something? We're gonna go fishing for the bandit? Bandit fishing?' My jaw dropped, excited. 'Oh, dibs! Band name! Called it! You can't use Bandit Fishing as a band name!'

Wyatt stared at me. 'No,' he said, annoyed. 'We're not *tying a string* to it. We're just gonna set it down and watch it until someone nabs it.'

I folded my arms, and grumbled, 'I liked the *fishing* idea better.'

'What do we do when we find the bandit?' Naomi asked. 'Just run after him?'

Another brilliant idea came to my mind. 'Oh!' I said. 'Once we figure out who the bandit is, we could find them during lunch! And then we can hide in the ceiling right above them until they open their milk carton. Once their milk carton is open, we'll lower a thread down into his drink, and then send a single drop of truth serum down the thread until it drips into their milk. After that, we'll confront the bandit in front of Principal Davis, and because of the truth serum, he'll spill his guts. Boom. Day saved *again* by the super handsome Chase Cooper. You lose, bandit, but thanks for playing.'

Naomi and Wyatt looked at me in disbelief.

'Sweet idea, right?' I asked, smiling smugly.

Naomi held her hand out and raised her index finger. 'One – hanging out in the ceiling of the cafeteria is probably asking for broken bones.' She put up a second finger. 'Two – even *if* truth serum was a real thing, we don't have access to it.' A third finger. 'Three – it would be *way* easier to just nab this crook instead of the plan you came up with.' Naomi's pinky finger joined the rest. 'And four – I'm concerned that if I wasn't here to put a stop to your *bonkers* plan, you and Wyatt would probably try to actually carry it out!'

'I think we'd stop once we couldn't get our hands on the truth serum,' Wyatt said.

I folded my arms and glanced to the side. 'Fine,' I said. 'I guess we'll just try to catch the kid.'

'Good,' Naomi said. 'Let's get started then, shall we?'

Wednesday.
The hallways.

Since the bandit was able to strike anywhere at any time, we figured there wasn't a bad place to set our trap. We chose the short hallway that wrapped around the front office. It was out of the way enough that we could remain hidden, but in an area where traffic was still pretty thick. It was perfect.

'Okay, one more time,' I said, staring into the bottom of the rubbish bin. 'We put the gum on that water fountain over there while I hide in this nasty bin over here, and when the bandit strikes, I jump out and catch him?'

We were behind the door to the janitor's closet, safely hidden from other students. Their shadows danced in the small opening at the bottom of the door.

Wyatt held his palms out. 'What's so difficult about that plan? Why do you keep repeating it like that?'

'It's just, I mean,' I said, trying to find the words. 'There's *gotta* be a more ninja way to do this.'

'What's more ninja than hiding in a rubbish bin?' Wyatt asked.

Naomi pressed her lips together and nodded at Wyatt. 'He's got a point.'

'Really?' I whined. 'You agree with *him*?'

'Honestly, I just want to see you sit in that rubbish bin,' Naomi lauged.

'I'm not even wearing my ninja mask,' I said.

Wyatt raised an eyebrow. 'Just because you're not wearing your ninja mask doesn't mean you're *not* a ninja.'

He made a good point.

'Now get in there, tiger,' Wyatt smirked.

I looked back into the bottom of the grey bin and saw all kinds of nasty half-eaten food and felt sorry for the janitors at the school. People could at least empty their soft drink cans before tossing them out!

I imagined, for a moment, the rise of the rubbish bins in the future. One day, they'll come to life and seek vengeance for all the gunk that people stuffed into them. Just remember, on the day it happens and bins begin devouring the human race because they're fed up, that I, Chase Cooper, *totally* called it.

I shut my eyes and mustered up some courage I had been saving for such an occasion.

'*So gross*,' I whispered as I set my feet into the bottom of the rubbish bin. I gripped the sides so I wouldn't slip on whatever mushy nastiness awaited me in the pit of the barrel.

Finally, I was completely crouched and tucked away like a ninja... hiding in a rubbish bin. Wyatt gently set the lid on top, but not without laughing at me first.

Naomi and Wyatt wheeled me across the hall to where our trap had been set by the water fountains.

Now all I had to do was wait.

Pushing up on the lid, I could see my pack of gum without giving away my position. Kids kept passing the bait, not even noticing it was there. A couple of kids even took sips from the fountains, but left the cinnamon gum alone!

At that point, I was starting to feel claustrophobic. The inside of the rubber barrel was getting hotter, and the stink of bananas and fish was overwhelming. At least if I needed to barf, I was in a good spot to do it.

And then it happened. I saw a hand reach out towards the pack of gum. I had to wait until the student had the gum in his hands before jumping out because they had to be caught red handed – with the pack of my gum in their possession.

The large hand touched the gum, and then the student pinched it with his fingers, lifting it into the air. Got him!

Who's throwing fish away in the hallway garbage???

I exploded out of the bin and grabbed the student's arm.

'*Ah-ha!*' I shouted, pointing my finger at the bandit's guilty face. '*Caught youuuuuuuuuuuu…*' I trailed off the second I realised it was Principal Davis's arm in my hand.

The principal stared at my finger. '*What's the meaning of this?*'

'Heh,' I laughed nervously, unable to release the principal's hand from my death grip. 'I um, that's uh, it's just some…ummm…'

'First of all,' the principal said, pulling his hand away from me, 'you're not allowed to have gum, so I'm taking this. Secondly, hiding at the bottom of a rubbish bin is probably never a good idea. And lastly, it looks like you've set a trap here.'

I wasn't sure what to say, so my brain automatically made me smile, totally making me look like completely guilty.

'You're not setting traps in school, are you, Chase?' Principal Davis asked with a groan.

Suddenly, Wyatt burst out of a door across the hall. 'Of course he's not setting a trap! He's helping me with a social experiment!'

The principal raised his eyebrows. 'Oh really?' he asked, suspicious.

To be fair, what we were doing *could* be considered a social experiment. I mean, we're baiting a thief to come out of hiding, hoping that the temptation was enough to trigger their evil desire.

Wyatt responded quickly. 'Yes! We wanted to see if the person who took this gum would take it to the lost and found.'

The principal's expression didn't change. He looked at Wyatt and then glanced at the pack of gum. 'Well, this *experiment* is over. You can't have gum anyway, so it wouldn't matter if they took it to the lost and found. They'd have just thrown it away.'

'Ah,' Wyatt said, smiling. 'Good to know. Thank you, sir. Have a great day.'

The principal squeezed the pack of gum in his hands and disappeared around the corner.

'Quick thinking,' Naomi said, joining us. She looked up at the clock on the wall. 'Whoops, gonna be late. We better get going.'

Wyatt helped me out of the bin. 'It's alright,' he said. 'We'll have to catch the bandit later today.'

I nodded, picking tiny pieces of rubbish off my clothing. 'Right,' I said. 'As long as *you're* in the bin next time.'

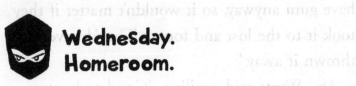

Wednesday.
Homeroom.

I was a little late to homeroom, so I had to sneak in. It took me a couple extra minutes to wipe my shoes off on the edge of the garbage can. All that trouble, and for nothing!

At the desk in front of me, Zoe sniffed at the air. '*Nasty!* What *is* that?'

I didn't say anything, hoping that maybe she was smelling something *other* than me.

My cousin turned around, disgusted. 'Ew, dude! Is that *you*? *What's all over your clothes?*'

'I was hiding in a rubbish bin—' I started to say.

'Because that's how *normal* kids start their day,' Zoe interrupted. 'I'm not sure that hanging out with Wyatt is working out for you.'

I was shocked. 'How... how did you know?'

'How'd we know you and Wyatt are buddy-buddy now?' Brayden asked, leaning closer. 'C'mon, man. We're not dumb. It's obvious. Plus Naomi said something to me yesterday about it.'

I closed my fist. '*Naomi!*'

'Um, no,' Zoe said. 'You're not allowed to be upset with her. She was just telling us because she's worried about you.'

'There's nothing to be worried about though!' I said, leaning back in my seat. Zoe was right; the stink of rubbish was lingering on me.

'There's not?' Zoe asked. 'Let's see, you're late to class and you reek like a dead skunk that came back to life and then died again. This is about all that gum that was stolen, isn't it?'

I didn't intentionally repeat Wyatt's words, but they came out anyway. 'Maybe,' I said. 'Maybe not.'

'Do I need to remind you that Wyatt and Sebastian are working together?' Zoe snipped. 'So while you're out saving the school from a gum bandit, *those* two are still up to something. And whatever it is probably ain't good!'

I thought about it for a moment. 'What if this is my chance to do something good *without* having to deal with costumed ninjas? And maybe my good influence can rub off on Wyatt. If that's the case, isn't it worth a shot?'

Zoe sighed, and looked me right in the eye. 'I get it,' she said. 'You're about honour and all that. I just don't want you to get in any kind of trouble. It's easier to get dragged down by someone than it is to pull them up.'

Zoe turned back to the front of the room. She was right, and I knew she was, but she didn't seem to understand that all I wanted to do was to find the gum bandit. At this point, it almost felt like an obsession.

I could overhear some conversations in class about how more gum had been stolen, so I knew the bandit was still out there. He just didn't happen to steal the gum we had tried to lure him with.

No matter though. It was still early, and there was plenty of time left in the day.

 **Wednesday.
Lunch.**

I stood outside the cafeteria, rolling the packet of gum in the palms of my hand. As students passed me to get in line for lunch, I watched their eyes to see if they looked at the bait in my hand. Too bad *every single kid* looked – kinda makes it hard to single anyone out as the bandit.

'I guess we're trying this again?' Naomi asked as she approached. She was a good ninja. A devoted ninja. I knew I could count on her.

I nodded. 'If Wyatt ever shows up.'

'Why wait for him?' Naomi asked. 'If he's late, it's his fault. You don't need him for any of this.'

She was right.

'Okay,' I said. 'Let's do this.'

'Where do we start?' Naomi asked, putting her hands on her hips and watching the students in line.

I pulled a piece of thread from my book bag. 'During art class, I managed to get a piece of string. I say we tie one end to the gum and the other end to my bag, and just wait. No garbage cans and no stinky mess. We don't even have to pay attention to the pack of gum! When the bandit takes it, the string will catch our attention!'

'*Bandit fishing*,' Naomi said.

'Bandit fishing,' I repeated, smiling.

Naomi helped me tie the string around the cinnamon gum pack while I secured the other end to one of the zippers on my bag. After the trap was set, we entered the cafeteria, but made sure to stay near the opening. If the bandit *were* to take the bait, the first thing he'd do would be run out of the cafeteria, so we wanted to make sure it would be easy to follow him out the doors.

I stuck the gum in the small pocket on the side of my book bag, just enough so that the end was visible. It was practically screaming to get stolen. I took a seat on the bench by the door. Naomi took the spot next to me.

'The other ninjas love the new hideout,' Naomi said, making conversation. 'But you've only been there once this week.'

Naomi was talking about the unused wrestling room I had stumbled upon a week ago. I was chasing Hotcakes, the penguin, through the school and ended up in that room. Part of me thinks Hotcakes *wanted* to show it to me. Since the room was unused, Coach Cooper said I was allowed to use it for a martial arts club. My ninja clan would have a legit place to train that would still be hidden from the rest of the school. It was perfect.

'I know I should be training with them,' I replied, 'but this situation has taken more attention from me than I wanted.'

Naomi nodded. 'You should still try to make

time for them. I mean, they're not only part of your ninja clan, they're your friends too.'

'I know, I know,' I whispered, feeling guilty. The truth was that I *wanted* to train with them. A sixth grade ninja who doesn't train is just a sixth grade kid.

At that moment, the zipper on my book bag flipped. I spun around, trying to get a look at the pack of gum, but it wasn't there anymore.

'Did you see who took it?' I asked, frantically jumping from the bench. 'It happened so quast that I didn't see anything!'

'No!' Naomi said. 'I was watching the cafeteria! Wait... what? What's *quast* mean?'

I felt like a dimwit. 'I meant to say 'quick', but at the last second tried to say 'fast'. So it came out as 'quast'.'

'Nice,' Naomi smiled.

My bag jerked to the left, pulling me along with it. The string was still attached to the gum! I plucked at the tight piece of thread, making the same sound as a guitar string. It was being pulled towards the staff entrance to the kitchen.

'Come on!' I said, racing along the wall, dodging students who were trying to find a seat with their food.

Naomi dashed past me like a bullet. She pulled the kitchen door open and we stepped through.

The kitchen was a hot mess of steam and food. The cooks were too busy moving tubs of spaghetti sauce back and forth to notice the two kids that had just walked through the door.

'This is why the bandit chose this exit,' I said. 'Everyone's distracted!'

'And the noise level is through the roof!' Naomi added, nearly shouting.

She was right. It was hard to hear *anything* over the voices of the cooks and the clanging pots and pans.

Naomi stepped forward and touched her finger to the string on my bag. It was still pulled tight, but not as tight as before. There was a little slack, which meant that the bandit had stopped running.

I followed Naomi as she jogged through the

kitchen. The smell of pasta and mashed potatoes was thick in the air as we turned the corner.

We were in the back of the kitchen now, where all the dry food was stored. Massive containers of mayonnaise, ketchup and mustard were stacked on shelves. Huge pallets of buns were set at the centre, and at the back of the room was another exit.

The white thread led from the zipper on my book bag to the floor, where it weaved around the pallet of buns and disappeared under the door at the back of the room. The string was completely loose at that point. The bandit had either stopped moving completely or had cut it. I was beginning to doubt we'd find him.

'Great,' I said, defeated. 'He's long gone by now.'

Naomi stepped forward. 'Maybe not,' she said, pointing at the string sticking out from under the door.

It was moving, but only slightly.

My heart started racing. 'He's still messing with the gum!' I said. 'The bandit is right on the other side of this door!'

Naomi grabbed the door handle and smiled at me. 'Are you ready for this?'

I swallowed hard and took a deep breath. 'Do it.'

Pushing the handle down, Naomi pulled the door open with all her strength.

I wasn't sure what I was expecting to see. In my head, I had always thought the bandit would look like a small mouse dressed in blue jeans, a white t-shirt and a leather jacket, with greased black hair and a stupid grin. I think I saw a movie like that once.

Instead, I saw the end of the piece of string lying on the ground. The bandit had cut the string.

All the hope and excitement that had built up inside me suddenly vanished, and I was left feeling empty.

'We weren't fast enough,' I said. 'We had him, but we just weren't *fast* enough!'

Naomi was by my side, but she didn't say anything.

'If we could've only been—'

Naomi nudged me with her elbow. 'Chase? You might wanna turn around now.'

Great. That was never a good thing to hear.

I looked over my shoulder to see what was spooking Naomi. Across the room, were three red ninjas – they always travel in packs of three.

'Lookie what we got here,' the ninja at the front sneered. 'A couple of kiddos who have lost their way.'

I narrowed my eyes. 'Jake?'

The ninja grabbed the bottom of his mask and ripped it off. His black hair flopped all over the place before it fell on his forehead.

It *was* Jake, and the two red ninjas behind him were probably members of his wolf pack.

Jake held his fist out at me. 'You hurt my leg this morning, and for that, you will *pay*.'

'That's a little extreme, isn't it?' Naomi asked.

'Not for a star football player!' one of the red ninjas behind Jake said. 'The team *needs* this guy, and you injured him!'

'It was an accident, and I said I was sorry!' I shouted.

'That doesn't mean there aren't consequences!' Jake said. He punched a fist into the palm of his hand. 'Get them!'

Part of a ninja's training involves learning how to use their surroundings to their advantage. A ninja has to be aware of everything around them at all times, so they can be prepared for anything, even if the only thing around them was a pallet of bread buns.

'Bun attack!' I shouted, grabbing handfuls of buns and chucking them across the room. I managed to get both of the red ninjas who were coming toward me. They flinched, stepping back towards Jake.

'He's throwing *bread* at you!' Jake shouted angrily.

Naomi grabbed the handle of the door behind us and pulled as hard as she could, but the door didn't budge. 'It's jammed! The only way out is *through* them!'

'Of course it is!' I replied. 'That's my luck, isn't it? James Buchanan is trying to ruin my life by trapping me in a kitchen with red ninjas!'

'You need serious help!' Naomi screamed, frustrated. Grabbing a handful of buns, she joined me, swinging her arm around like she was pitching a softball. The two red ninjas stuck their chests out and started marching towards Naomi and me. They knew the door behind us was stuck so they weren't in any hurry to beat the living tar out of us.

'It's been an honour to serve with you, sir,' Naomi said, way more serious than I think she meant to.

'We're not out of the game yet!' I said, balling one of the rolls into a tight wad of bread. 'Check *this* out!'

I threw it at one of the red ninjas as hard as I could. The ball of bread zoomed through the air so fast that it made a *fssshhhh* sound. Time seemed to stand still as the bun drew closer and closer to the red ninja's face. I could see the fear in his eyes. He wanted to panic, but his brain wasn't fast enough to make his body respond.

Closer and closer until ... it sailed over his head.

Naomi slapped her forehead. 'This is how I die.'

The two red ninjas approached with their fists in the air. Naomi took a step back, planting her feet firmly on the ground. I did the same, waiting for the attack.

Suddenly, the door behind us burst open, flooding the room with sunlight. The two ninjas stumbled around, blinded. They covered their faces, shielding their eyes from the light.

A figure stood tall in the doorway as sunlight washed over it. It was impossible to see their face.

'The white ninja?' Naomi whispered, squinting her eyes.

'I don't know,' I said. It was still difficult to see, but it was obvious that the figure was wearing some sort of one-piece costume. The outline looked almost the same as a clown's outfit. Was Miko standing in the doorway?

'Leave them alone!' the shadowed figured commanded.

'Miko, is that you?' I asked, squinting. 'Are you wearing your clown outfit?'

'Clowns!' Jake said quickly. 'No! No clowns! *No clowns!*'

The two red ninjas looked at each other confused.

'I *hate* clowns!' Jake shouted as he tripped over his feet. 'They're unnatural! Why would anyone ever want to paint their face like that? *Why?*'

The two red ninjas ran to him and helped him to his feet.

'Ninjas!' Jake shouted. 'Vanish!'

One of the ninjas pulled out a sack filled with chalk dust and slammed it on the ground. When the dust had cleared, all three red ninjas were gone.

I spun around, ready to confront whoever was standing in the door. 'Miko?' I asked again cautiously.

The figure stepped into the kitchen and shut the door behind him. Naomi's jaw hit the floor when she saw his face.

It was Wyatt and he was wearing overalls.

'No way,' I said to myself. Did Wyatt really just save the day? Had he seriously turned over a new leaf? Like, for real?

Wyatt acted like it wasn't a big deal. 'That was crazy, huh? Did you ever get that box of erasers to the front office like I asked you to?'

I shook my head in disbelief. Even though Wyatt saved us, it didn't change the fact that members of *his* red ninja clan were trying to hurt us.

'Those were *your* ninjas!' I said, ignoring his question.

Wyatt nodded, setting his hands on his hips like he was disappointed. 'I know, I know. What a bunch of jerks, right?'

I stared at Wyatt for a moment, my mind completely blown. '*Are you kidding me?*'

'What?' Wyatt said, annoyed.

'Those guys are on *your* team!'

Scratching the back of his head, Wyatt said, 'Too bad they were wearing their masks or else we'd know who it was.'

'It was Jake!' Naomi said. 'Jake didn't have his mask on!'

'Jake?' Wyatt asked, looking a little more than confused as he walked across the room. 'Man, I've had problems with that kid since ... well, since he joined my clan.'

Biting my lip, I stared toward the direction Jake and his wolf pack ran off in.

'Wait,' Wyatt said suddenly. 'You don't suppose ...'

I glanced at Wyatt, waiting for him to finish.

'You don't think *he's* the bandit, do you?'

I looked back at the exit and saw my string leading out the door. 'No. He came in *after* we followed the bandit back here.'

'You ...' Wyatt said softly. 'Followed the bandit back here? Did you *see* the bandit?'

Naomi stepped forwards. 'For all we know, the bandit is *you*. The gum was taken out the exit door, and the string was *also* cut out there!

And then *who* happens to use that door to save us?'

Wyatt put his hands up. 'I can tell you right now that I'm *not* the bandit. Remember? I was sitting with Chase the first day the bandit even struck!'

I looked at Naomi, nodding. She folded her arms and scowled at the floor.

'But,' Wyatt continued, 'Jake just happened to be back here after you lost the bandit? Doesn't that sound *too* coincidental? I mean, look around! Why would he hang out in the kitchen?'

'I don't know,' Naomi said. 'Why are *you* hanging out in the kitchen? And wearing those ridiculous overalls?'

Wyatt pulled the denim straps on his shoulders proudly. 'I'm volunteering my time back here. I was out taking the rubbish, which is why I was outside.'

'Volunteering?' I asked.

'I'm the vice president now,' Wyatt sighed. 'I've got to do things like this to look good.'

I chuckled.

Naomi pressed her lips together and looked at me. 'He's got a point. Why would Jake and his wolf pack even be back here?'

It didn't make sense, that's for sure. Jake and his red ninjas had no reason to hang out in the kitchen at all, so the fact that they suddenly appeared *right after* we lost the bandit was something to think about.

But if the red ninjas were the ones behind the thefts, then Wyatt would *have* to have something to do with it too, wouldn't it? How would the leader of the red ninjas not have a clue about what his clan was doing?

If Wyatt was in on it, then that meant he was playing me, right? But how can Wyatt be in on it if *he's* the one who suggested it was Jake in the first place?

Seriously! It felt like my brain was crying! I was beginning to feel like all of this was a little too much to handle on my own. Naomi had been by my side the entire time, but even *she* warned me about getting involved in the first place.

Maybe my friends were right. Maybe I shouldn't have taken on this case when I did. No one else in the school seemed to care. Maybe I shouldn't either.

Wednesday.
The careers fair.

I sat at my seat in the cafeteria when the careers fair started. All around me were other students laughing and having a good time with their mentors. Even Brayden looked like he was having fun with the guy in the wolf costume.

Zoe was mixing glasses of lemonade with her mentor. Faith was looking at a laptop screen with hers. I swear, if I saw a ninja mentoring some other kid in this room, I was gonna lose it.

'Howdy, kiddo!' Miko said as he flopped his huge red feet towards me, each step slapping the ground like an oversized flapjack.

I smiled tightly, not even trying to make it look genuine. 'Sup,' I said nodding once in the clown's general direction.

Miko sat next to me. After a moment, he spoke again, but using his normal voice. 'So hey, there's this kid I keep seeing around here. His left calf muscle is bigger than his right one, and I mean like, *scary* big. Like that was the only part of his body that he decided to work out.'

'Oh, Brian?' I asked.

The clown stared at me. 'Um, if *Brian* has a monster hiding in his left leg then, yes, Brian. What's his deal?'

'He broke the right pedal off his bicycle at the beginning of the year,' I explained. 'He keeps saying he's gonna replace it, but I think he likes the attention. Plus he keeps going around telling everyone he's super ripped, even if it's only in one calf.'

'Seriously,' Miko said, shaking his head. 'If he kicked me with that leg, I'd probably have to go to the hospital.'

I laughed.

Miko took notice that my guard was down. 'Want to hear a joke?'

'Hit me,' I said.

'Knock, knock,' Miko said.

Wonderful. A classically boring knock-knock joke. 'Who's there?' I asked.

'Banana.'

'Banana who?'

Miko snickered, covering his nose. 'Banana you glad I didn't say ban ... wait, I messed that up. Let me start over. Knock, knock.'

It was easily the worst joke I'd ever heard, and the fact that he messed it up should've made it *less* funny, but it got me, and I laughed out loud. It was actually kinda nice to take my mind off Jake, the wolf pack and the Buchanan bandit.

Miko sighed and leaned back against the table. He pulled a can of soft drink from one of his oversized pockets and popped it open, letting it fizz over a little. It was an orange soft drink, which happened to be my favourite in the entire history of canned beverages.

'What's your deal?' I said. 'Did you lose a bet or something?'

Miko looked a little annoyed. 'Why? Because I'm a clown?'

I nodded. 'Yeah. Did your friends bet you wouldn't go through with it?'

'Actually,' Miko said, 'all my friends are clowns too.'

I let out a short laugh. 'Yeah? That's something I'd like to see,' I said sarcastically. 'You should get *all* your clown buddies to perform on Friday. That'd be totes cool.'

The clown raised his eyebrows. 'I didn't lose a bet. I *chose* this job.'

'But why?' I asked, sitting forward. 'That's what I don't understand! Why would you *choose* such a lame job?'

'Because I love doing it,' Miko said after a pause.

'Typical answer,' I said.

'If you'd quit being such a thick toenail for a second, maybe you'd see that I was telling the truth,' Miko said.

'You love wearing too much make-up and an outfit that looks like you're just wearing a tent?' I joked.

'I love performing and I love making people laugh,' Miko said. 'I love see someone genuinely laugh until they cry. Making people happy, even if it's just for a second, is the reason why I do this. But more importantly, if I didn't love doing it, I'd be doing something else.'

I stopped to think for moment. Miko was right, and I felt bad. 'I'm sorry,' I said. 'I've just got a lot on my plate right now.'

'Yeah?' Miko said. 'What could a sixth grader possibly be stressing about?'

I looked Miko in the eye. 'Just because I'm in sixth grade doesn't mean my life is all rainbows and gumdrops. Just 'cause I go to school all day and play video games all night doesn't mean I'm *not* dealing with some things.'

It was Miko who apologised this time. 'Sorry, man,' he said softly. 'You're right. Problems are problems, no matter who you are.'

I nodded. 'Thanks,' I said, feeling

embarrassed. 'So this clown thing... You really love doing it, huh?'

'Sure do,' Miko said without missing a beat.

I sighed. 'I can see that in you, I really can. I'm actually a little jealous that I can't make that kind of decision.'

'What kind of decision?' Miko asked.

'Y'know, just to live life without caring what anyone else thinks,' I said, gesturing to everyone in the room. 'As a sixth grader, I feel like my entire life is sometimes controlled by what's cool and what's not.'

'What you *think* is cool,' Miko said, correcting me. 'That's where the difference is, and it's a *huge* difference.'

I looked at the clown, confused. 'What do you mean?'

Miko sat quietly for a second, observing the other students. And then he answered. 'Be inspired by the things you love – not by the things you *think* you should love.'

'Huh?' I said.

'Like, I remember when I was your age, I was

really into comic books – superhero comics especially,' Mike said.

I nodded. 'Right. Me too.'

'Well,' Miko said, 'I kind of got made fun of for it because I'd always have a stack of comics in my backpack. While other dudes were writing notes to girls, I had my face buried in the latest issue of my favourite comic.'

I kept nodding. 'What's that got to do with—'

'Can I finish?' Miko asked, a little annoyed.

'Sorry.'

'After being made fun of for a while, I took a little break from comics. Nobody was ever really *mean*, but they still said things, y'know? Jokes about when I'd grow up and get a girlfriend or something.'

I totally understood. 'Even a tiny comment can ruin my day.'

'Exactly!' Miko said. 'All that happened was that someone shook their head at me and called me immature. That's all they said, but that was it for me. I stopped reading comics for years because of that.'

I sat forward, resting my elbows on my knees. 'Man...'

'I know, right?' Miko said. 'It took a few years before I realised that I really missed reading comics. Like, a lot.'

'That's *lame* though,' I said. 'You shouldn't have stopped reading them in the first place if you loved them so much! Who *cares* what other people think? Comic books are harmless, and if they bring a little bit of joy to you, then read 'em! But that's not even talking about *just* comics! Like, you shouldn't be ashamed about *anything* you love, especially if...oh...I get it.'

Miko pointed at me and smiled. 'Bingo.'

'Whoa,' I whispered. 'You just blew my mind.'

Miko chuckled.

'I just wish it were that easy,' I added, watching the kids in the cafeteria.

Miko sighed. 'It never is.'

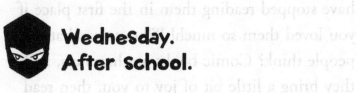

Wednesday.
After school.

I met Zoe outside the side doors of the school. Since we live pretty close to each other, her dad gives me a ride home too. She was sitting at a picnic table under the shade of a giant tree.

'Whatcha doing?' I asked, setting my book bag on the table.

'Texting,' Zoe replied. 'Faith is coming over later tonight for dinner. Oh! Ask your parents if you can come too! It'll be fun!'

Zoe was my cousin. Every Sunday our families get together for brunch, usually taking turns to host each week. Every now and then,

we all hang out on a weeknight too, so I'm sure
my parents would let me go to Zoe's for dinner.

'I'll ask,' I said, staring at the table, watching
the shadows of leaves as they trembled in the
breeze.

Zoe set her phone down and folded her
hands. She wanted me to know I had her full
attention. 'What's the matter?'

I didn't say anything.

'It's this thing with Wyatt, isn't it?'

Again, I didn't say anything.

'Look at how you're acting,' Zoe said. 'It's clearly affecting you.'

'It's not *just* Wyatt,' I said finally. 'It's also the gum bandit. It's Jake and his wolf pack. It's all the homework I haven't done yet. It's Miko and his life lessons. It's whatever Sebastian is planning with Wyatt. It's Faith. It's Naomi. It's just ... it's everything at the same time right now. *All of it.* The whole world seems to be resting on my shoulders.'

'I think that maybe you're taking on too much this time,' Zoe said. 'I mean, I understand that you feel like you need to do something about the bandit, but really, I think it's Wyatt that's dragging you down the most out of all that stuff.'

'I know,' I admitted.

'It's not easy hanging out with people like that,' Zoe said. 'At least not when you're complete opposites, y'know? I used to have this friend here, I mean, she still goes here, but we hardly ever talk anymore. I think I've said maybe one word to her this entire year.'

'What happened?' I asked.

'She fell in with a different crowd,' Zoe said, shrugging. 'At first it was alright, but the more I hung out with her, the more I felt myself changing too. She was never a negative person before, but after she started hanging out with these kids, she suddenly became all drama. *Drama drama drama.* All she ever did was talk smack about pretty much everyone, and complain about everything. She just became so ... *ugly* on the inside.'

'What did you do?' I asked.

'I tried to stay friends with her,' Zoe replied. 'My parents said that she probably needed someone positive in her life, but after a little while, I just couldn't do it anymore. This one time she texted me to ask if I had been invited to someone's birthday party – I guess she saw a bunch of pictures posted online or something. When I told her I wasn't invited, she said, *Good, I just wanted to make sure I wasn't the only one. LOL.*'

'Wow,' I said, floored.

'Yeah,' Zoe said, nodding. 'Seriously, I'm alright with not getting invited to parties. I get it. Sometimes they're just for a certain group of friends, or maybe even family. But that text made me feel like I was being left out on purpose. It made me feel sick. I sometimes wonder if she wanted me to feel bad so she wasn't alone.'

Zoe's dad pulled up. He honked twice and waved.

'You're right,' I said, grabbing my book bag. 'I'm done with Wyatt.'

Zoe didn't say anything. She didn't have to. I could tell she was proud.

Instead, she punched me in the arm the way buddies do. But Zoe liked to mix it up sometimes, and this time she threw a really hard punch. I winced, laughing the pain off and acting like it didn't hurt, but I'm pretty sure it was going to bruise.

**Thursday.
Before School.**

The next morning was the same story – the gum bandit had struck again, and only the students knew. If any of the teachers overheard conversations in the hallways, then *maybe* they were aware of the stealing spree, but if they had heard, they sure didn't show any signs of knowing.

Here's the weird thing though – almost everyone was *chewing on gum*.

That's right. As I made my way through the students in the hallway, it was easier to count how many kids weren't chewing on gum. It was like there was more of it since the bandit started on Monday. Maybe kids were so afraid of getting their gum stolen that they chewed on it instead of leaving it in their bags.

Suddenly, Wyatt appeared by my side. It's creepy how good he is at that.

'What's the plan for today?' he asked.

'What do you mean?' I replied.

'I mean, how are we gonna bust this bandit?'

'Look, I've been thinking a lot about it, and I think I'm just gonna give up on the whole thing.'

Wyatt looked angry. 'But you can't! Not when you're this close! I mean, not when *we're* this close!'

'How do you think we're close?' I asked.

'Jake!' Wyatt yelled. 'Jake was there in the kitchen yesterday! He *has* to be the bandit!'

'But if it's Jake, then maybe I *should* quit pressing the issue,' I said. 'Seems like he's playing the role of the new bully in school, and that's not exactly a show I'd like to be a part of.'

'But if you bust him, you can be the hero!' Wyatt said. 'Again!'

I stopped in the middle of the hallway. 'If it's so important to you, why don't *you* bust him?'

Wyatt stumbled over some words, but stopped immediately. He stepped closer to me and whispered as if he were telling a secret. 'Because I'm the vice president, and that's enough attention for me. I've become happy being the guy who's behind the scenes. Y'know?'

'And here I thought you'd settle for nothing less than the lead,' I said, suspicious.

Wyatt grinned, placing his hand on my shoulder and pushing me along. 'Seriously,' he said quietly. 'I'm *trying* to be a better person, and I see this whole situation as my test. If I can help bust the bandit and make it so that *you're* the hero, then I feel like the universe will reward me for it. I think it's called karma.'

'So you think if you do good things, then good things will happen to you?' I asked.

Wyatt nodded.

I sighed, still feeling unchanged about the situation. I brushed his hand off my shoulder, and continued to walk without him.

'I'm out,' I said confidently. 'There's
something about all this that's making my skin
crawl, and I need to trust my instinct.'

Wyatt didn't follow me. He remained
perfectly still in the middle of the hallway. I
knew he was staring daggers at me, but I didn't
care. I had made my decision.

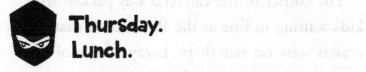 **Thursday.
Lunch.**

I was feeling great about my decision to leave the bandit behind. It was more trouble than it was worth, and the whole thing would blow over anyway. Everyone would forget that the bandit even existed after the week was over.

As I walked into the cafeteria, I scanned the room for my friends. A lot of the mentors were already there, talking to one another, waiting for the fair to start. They were all wearing special badges around their necks as a sign that they were allowed to be in the school.

155

Finally, I saw Faith sitting at a table on her own. When she saw me, she smiled.

Cutting a path across the lunchroom, I couldn't help but notice that most of the students had stacks of Sebastian's colourful erasers displayed proudly in front of them.

The corner of the cafeteria was packed with kids waiting in line at the Pit, excited that the erasers were on sale there. Every couple of seconds, someone would walk away from the shop hollering about how they managed to get their hands on one. It reminded me of a midnight release at a video game shop.

Jake and his wolf pack were sitting on the stage at the front of the cafeteria, eating their lunch and pointing at random kids, probably making jokes about their clothing or something.

I took the seat across from Faith. A voice came from behind me. 'Chase?'

A young guy carrying a duffel bag was walking through the cafeteria toward me. I didn't recognise him. 'Yeah?' I asked.

'It's *me*,' the man said, stopping in place and holding out his hands. 'Miko!'

Without the make-up, he looked like a completely normal dude. 'Hey, uh ... Miko. Is Miko your real name?'

The clown set his duffel bag on the floor and took a seat next to me. 'It sure is.'

'So you're Chase's mentor for the week, huh?' Faith asked.

Miko nodded, setting a golden bicycle horn on the table. I lowered my head, embarrassed.

'Before I get my gear on,' Miko said, 'I wanted to let you know that a bunch of my friends will be here tomorrow. I told Principal Davis your idea about us performing on Friday and he *loved* it.'

'*What?*' I said. 'Dude, I was *joking!*'

Miko was unfazed. 'Oh? Huh. Well, they'll still be here tomorrow afternoon to put on a killer show.'

I shook my head, watching Faith's reaction from the corner of my eye. 'Sounds *kind* of alright,' I said, trying to be cool.

'I think it sounds *fun*,' Faith said.

Miko sat up and smiled. 'Thaaaank you,' he said, and then he jerked his thumb at me. 'Try telling *this* guy to lighten up a little.'

'Dude, I'm already light,' I said defensively. 'I'm the lightest guy in the room, alright? I'm so light, I'm bright!'

Faith took a bite of her fries. 'You're doing that thing where you make no sense.'

I lowered my head, but didn't say anything. I looked on the stage and saw Jake pointing and chuckling at me. Great. Now they're making fun of *me*.

Miko must've seen how embarrassed I felt because he grabbed his duffel bag and stood up. He patted my shoulder once, and said, 'See ya at the fair, kiddo.'

Once he left, Faith laughed a little. 'That guy seems pretty cool.'

'Really?' I asked. 'An adult that chose to be a clown seems cool to you?'

'Totes,' she said with a mouthful of fries. 'So what if he's a clown? He's probably just doing what he loves, a lot like a good friend of mine. He goes around the school wearing *ninja* clothes under his street clothes. He's even got a secret ninja clan that he trains with sometimes in some secret part of the school.'

I raised my hands, surrendering. 'I get it,' I said.

Faith took a swig from her orange juice. 'We're all just doing what we love, aren't we?'

Just then, someone bumped into my back. I turned, expecting to see Miko again, but when I looked, there was nobody there.

'Sorry about that,' said a boy further down the aisle. The boy was wearing a hat so I couldn't see his face.

'No big deal,' I said, waving at him.

The boy didn't turn around, but waved back at me as he passed some students at the end of our table. They were busy stacking their colourful erasers in a line and knocking them over like dominos.

I caught a glimpse of Jake and the wolf pack again. They had finished their lunches and were throwing erasers at each other, like little kids trying to prove how hard they could throw something.

'Where are all your erasers?' I asked Faith.

She looked at the group of kids. 'I could ask you the same question.'

'I don't really know anything about them,' I said. 'I've been too busy with the whole bandit thing.'

Faith nodded, understanding. 'Well, I bought a couple, but they weren't worth their weight in dollars. They're *terrible* erasers. They just smudged all my stuff instead of actually doing what they were supposed to do.'

'Everybody seems to be in love with them,' I said. 'And you gotta admit, they *do* come in some pretty funky colours.'

'If I cared about brightly coloured rubber bricks, then I guess I'd have a whole stack of them to show off too, wouldn't I?' Faith said.

That was the best part about Faith. It didn't matter what everyone else was doing – she made her own decisions about things, and the fact that she didn't have any erasers meant she didn't care if people thought she was lame for not having any.

'I guess so,' I said, casually looking around the students in the cafeteria. I swung my feet around to face away from the table, but something caught my foot. There was a small red book bag leaning against the table leg.

'Is this your bag?' I asked Faith.

Faith leaned over and looked under the table. 'Nuh-uh,' she said. 'Is there a name on it?'

I hoisted the bag onto the lunch table, and

inspected it. The zipper on the back unzipped a few inches from the weight of whatever was inside. 'Not that I can see,' I said, spinning the bag around. 'It's heavy though.'

'What's in it?' Faith asked.

'Books, probably,' I joked, peeking into the opening on the side of the bag.

Suddenly I caught a whiff of spearmint. The smell was so strong that I flinched. And then I saw what was inside the bag.

It was filled with packs of gum.

I immediately pushed the bag shut and held it close to my chest.

'What is it?' Faith asked, concerned. 'What's in the bag?'

'Nothing!' I replied right away. 'It's *empty*.'

'No it's not,' Faith said, poking one corner of the book bag. 'It's filled with *something*.'

I was so freaked that I spoke without thinking. 'Corn dogs! It's just a book bag filled with corn dogs! That's all! There's no incriminating evidence inside this bag that mysteriously showed up at my feet!'

I spun around in my seat and desperately searched for the kid who'd bumped into me. It *must* have been him! Why didn't I pay more attention? I even talked to him! I *talked* to the Buchanan bandit! He was in the palm of my hands and I let him get away!

'Chase, what's your problem?' Faith asked, leaning across the table and reaching for the bag. 'Show me what's going on!'

I jumped up and pulled the straps over my shoulders. 'I know whose bag it is!' I said, lying. 'So I'm just gonna head to the principal's office and drop it off! They'll probably make an announcement about it being in the front office or something.'

'Chase!' Faith said, frustrated and reaching across the table for me. 'Sit down!'

'Lates!' I said, saluting her. I turned and scrambled to the front of the cafeteria, keeping an eye out for the boy who ran into me. Was it

Jake? No, he was still on the stage when it happened. Unless he was some sort of teleporting alien, it couldn't have been him. But that doesn't mean it wasn't a member of his wolf pack.

I shuffled into the school lobby, unsure of my next move. I saw Principal Davis walk out of the front offices with Coach Cooper and I panicked. I had enough evidence on my back to put me in detention for life, and I wasn't about to get caught with it.

Hanging a hard left, I headed for the boys' restroom down the hallway. It was the restroom with a million different exits, one to the hallway, one to the boys' locker room, one to the gymnasium, and one to the cafeteria. If I got in a bind in there, at least I wouldn't be trapped in a corner.

I pushed the door open with my shoulder and stepped inside. There was a boy washing his hands at the sink. He looked at me in the mirror.

'Howdy!' I said.

My brain started screaming at me. *What's the matter with you? Who says 'howdy'? In fact, who even makes conversation in a restroom at all?? Are you trying to get yourself caught? Eyes on the floor and don't say another word!*

The boy nodded, and pumped the soap dispenser.

When I'm nervous, it's impossible for me to keep my mouth shut.

'Washing your hands, huh?' I asked, pointing at the sink. 'Yeah, you'll really want to get that soap all bubbly. Did you know it's actually the *bubbles* that clean the dirt off you? True story.'

Stop it! He knows how to wash his hands!

And then I pointed to the air dryer on the wall. 'You can dry them off over there, good sir.'

You're being weird right now, even for you.

'Um, thanks?' the boy said, raising his voice like he was asking a question. 'But I prefer paper towels.'

'Excellent choice,' I said, watching as he pulled the brown paper towels out of the metal box on the wall.

165

Finally, he left the restroom and I was alone. I went into one of the stalls near the back and locked the door. I got up enough courage to look inside the bag again.

There had to be hundreds of packs of stolen gum, crammed into the canvas bag. Sitting on top of the pile was a folded sheet of paper.

I took it in my hands and unfolded it, expecting another threat, but instead it read:

Kind regards, the wolf pack.

It *was* the wolf pack.

A small chirp came from inside the bag, and then the loudest siren I've ever heard started going off. The wolf pack had set me up with a bag of stolen goods and an alarm to get everyone's attention!

I freaked.

Stumbling back, I fell against the stall door and steadied myself. The alarm was so loud that my head started hurting. I thrust my hand into the bag and felt the small siren at the bottom, but it was attached to the lining of the bag.

I couldn't remove it so I did the next best thing – I stuffed the book bag into the toilet bowl, splashing toilet water all over the place, hoping the siren would short out from getting wet.

'Oh my god,' I said, clenching my teeth. 'I hope the last person who used this flushed!'

The blaring siren became muffled and started bubbling, but it was still going off. I gripped the bag tighter and thrashed it around at the bottom of the toilet until finally, it shut off.

I stood frozen, catching my breath, soaking wet, with my hands gripping a backpack that I had just stuffed into a toilet. Easily one of my top five worst moments at Buchanan, maybe even my entire life.

I dragged the wet bag on the floor behind me as I stepped out of the stall. I didn't feel like things could get much worse.

I was wrong.

One of the restroom doors creaked open, and Principal Davis's voice echoed across the tiles. 'What in the *world* is going on in here? Who's back there?'

I ran to the side entrance behind the stalls, hoping that it would lead to the boys' locker room. Kicking the wooden door open, I jumped through carrying the wet book bag over my shoulders.

Stumbling over my feet, I fell to the floor, squeezing my eyes shut, afraid of getting hurt. The book bag slid to my side, dragging me along with it because of how heavy it was, and I rolled onto my back. I heard a few packets of gum bounce out of the bag, and then everything fell silent. I was glad too because I wasn't sure if I had chosen the correct door, but the fact that there weren't any other sounds made me feel better... until I opened my eyes...

... and saw the upside-down faces of other sixth graders staring at me, the boy who just exploded out of the bathroom, dripping with water.

I was in the cafeteria, to the right of the stage. I saw Jake and his wolf pack glaring at me. When Jake saw the packs of gum on the floor, his eyes bulged.

Hopping off the stage, he started to speak, but I picked myself up and cut him off.

'*Jake's* the one who's been stealing everyone's gum!' I shouted. 'And he's been trying to set me up the entire time!'

Jake stopped and looked shocked. His mouth was open, but he didn't say anything.

'See?' I said, pointing at him. I dropped the book bag. It hit the cold floor with a gross splat. I unzipped it, flipped it over, and dumped hundreds of wet packs of gum onto the ground.

Everyone in the cafeteria gasped.

Wyatt suddenly appeared at the front of the onlookers, staring at all the gum on the floor. President Sebastian was right behind him, wearing a disgruntled looked on his face.

Jake remained silent, which surprised me, but the colour of his face did a good job of letting everyone know he was getting angrier.

Again, I accused him. 'He's been doing this all week! *He's* the gum bandit!'

Principal Davis stepped forward, looking me up and down, probably wondering why I was soaked to the bone. He looked at Jake and said, 'Even though gum isn't allowed here, doesn't make it okay to take it.' And then the principal addressed the crowd of students. 'Has this been going on all week?'

Many of the students mumbled together.

'Why hasn't anyone said anything?' Principal Davis asked. He turned back to Jake. 'Is this true? Are you stealing from your peers?'

Jake's face was as red as a beetroot. I expected steam to shoot from his ears.

'No!' Jake shouted. 'It's not true! I mean, *yes*, I did it, but I was doing it because *wha—*'

'*Whyyyyy* can't you simply take the blame for what you've done?' Wyatt said, cutting Jake's sentence off. 'You've stolen everyone's gum. It doesn't matter that gum isn't even allowed in school. What matters is that *you* and *your wolf pack* are the Buchanan bandits.'

Jake's clenched his fists, but he didn't argue. He shook his head, glaring at Wyatt, and then he looked at Sebastian for a moment as if waiting for the president to say something.

Sebastian lowered his gaze and turned away. Things were quiet, and honestly pretty awkward.

It was weird.

Jake stepped forward and said, '*Why aren't you—*'

Sebastian pointed his finger in the air. 'To detention with you!'

Jake bit his lip, but said nothing else.

Principal Davis raised an eyebrow. 'Thank you, Sebastian, but how about letting *me* handle this?'

Sebastian smiled. 'Of course, I'm sorry. I got carried away. You may take him away now.'

The principal shook his head, sighing. 'I've had a long day, Sebastian, please don't make it any longer.'

Sebastian nodded, flashing his award-winning smile.

Principal Davis gestured for two of the hall monitors to clean up the book bag mess. Jake and his wolf pack had to leave the cafeteria for questioning. Wyatt and Sebastian stood in the corner, deep in conversation.

173

The principal approached me. 'I'll have a couple of questions for you in a little bit, Chase.'

'How come?' I asked.

The principal shot me a stern look. 'Because you're soaking wet with a bag *full* of stolen gum! Do you honestly think I'd miss a detail like that? You're obviously involved in all this somehow, and depending on what Jake says, I'll have more than a few words for you too.'

I lowered my head. 'Right.'

Principal Davis sighed. 'I know it's been a rough couple of months here,' he said softly. 'But I'm just trying to make sure you're not mixing with the wrong crowd.'

'Like chocolate milk and lemonade?'

'Like what?' The principal asked.

I shook my head. 'Nothing.'

Principal Davis walked out of the cafeteria. One of the hall monitors handed me a towel to dry myself off. Taking a seat on the stage, I ran the towel through my wet hair.

Faith, Brayden, Gavin and Zoe sat beside me,

watching as everyone began setting up for the career fair.

Faith was the first to speak. 'So was that whole thing weird, or was it just me?'

Zoe nodded. 'It was weird alright, but why? The bandit was busted and the day was saved, wasn't it?'

Brayden shrugged. 'Is it weird because we want it to be weird? Maybe in this case it really was as simple as it turned out to be.'

'It feels like it was too easy,' Gavin said, staring at nothing. 'But I say take what you can get.'

My friends all nodded, but I wasn't so sure I felt the same. 'Jake might've been the gum bandit all week, but he wasn't the one who planted the book bag by my feet.'

Faith looked up. 'But you never saw who dropped it, did you?'

'No,' I said. 'But I saw Jake on the stage about a second after that kid bumped into me.'

'What kid?' Zoe asked.

'Someone bumped into Chase's back and

apparently dropped the backpack full of stolen gum by his feet,' Faith explained.

Zoe rolled her eyes. 'Of course they did. I forgot this was *Chase* we were talking about.'

I laughed. 'But Jake was on the stage when that kid dumped the bag by me, so it couldn't have been him. It's like someone's trying to frame Jake, which means somebody's trying to frame him *framing me*, if you can wrap your head around that.'

'Why'd you accuse Jake to begin with then?' Brayden asked.

'There was a note in the bag,' I said. 'And it was signed 'the wolf pack'.'

'There it is,' Gavin said, nodding. 'It wasn't Jake that put the bag there, he got one of his minions to do it instead. Jake *was* behind it all the entire time. Sometimes you can get caught in a circle if you *over*analyse things, y'know?'

Just then, President Sebastian raised his arms and started speaking loudly. 'We've all had a pretty crazy week here at Buchanan School, but I think we can now rest easy knowing that the bandit has been caught!' He smiled and pumped his first toward me like he was giving a speech. 'And we have our very own Chase Cooper to thank for bringing the criminal to justice! Everyone give Chase a hand!'

The students clapped at the president's command.

Sebastian continued. 'I wish I could hand out gum to celebrate Chase's heroism, but alas, the school *doesn't* allow gum.'

A few kids moaned, 'Awwww.'

Sebastian shut his eyes and held his hand in the air, waiting for everyone to quiet down. 'But that doesn't mean we can't celebrate some *other* way. For the rest of the day, and *today only*, my erasers will be *fifty* per cent off!'

The entire cafeteria exploded in applause. It's possible that a couple kids died of heart attacks – probably not, but they sure were acting like they were going to. I think I even saw someone in the back gasping into a brown paper bag.

'Get your own eraser right now in the Pit!' Sebastian shouted, but was barely able to get his voice above the shouting crowd. 'Check out the new colour 'wacky watermelon'! It *smells* just like watermelon!'

Zoe groaned. 'Leave it to him to take this situation and make money off it.'

'Oh well,' I said. 'As long as all the attention is off me, I'm happy.'

I sat on the stage as my friends went back to their tables for the career fair. Nothing was adding up in my head no matter how I tried spinning the story, but maybe Gavin was right – it's possible that I was trying too hard to figure everything out when it was already figured out.

So why was my gut telling me something was still jacked up?

**Friday.
Before school.**

I got to school the next day hoping that
everything would be back to normal. For all
the other students, it probably was, but they
also didn't know about the week I had just
gone through. In fact, most of the kids here
don't have a clue about *anything* that goes on
behind their backs. It's probably better that way.

As I walked to my locker, I couldn't help but
notice the sound of incessant gum chomping.
It was impossible to shut out the *slurpy slurp*
sounds coming from nearly every kid I passed.
Man, and I thought pirate jargon was annoying?

This was turning out to be a hundred times worse! I guess with the bandit behind detention doors, everyone kind of went crazy with their gum.

What made it worse was that I was more tired than a sheep after getting sheared. Wait, sheep don't have to do anything when getting sheared, so maybe they're not tired after that. Whatever – you get it.

I didn't sleep the best overnight, I kept tossing and turning. I really wish I was the kind of kid who could push these thoughts out of my mind, but I just wasn't. It's my curse.

'*Grandmaster Chase!*' Faith said, meeting me by my locker. 'What's crackin'?'

I spun my locker combination into the dial and swung the door open, leaning into the opening so all the rubbish in the lower half didn't fall out. 'I'm still bugged by all this,' I said.

Faith sighed, leaning against the locker next to mine. She watched the other students in the hallway.

'Everyone seems to be cool this morning,' she

said. 'Nobody has to worry about getting stuff stolen and they seem to be enjoying their new erasers. The world has returned to normal.'

Faith was right. Nearly everyone in the hallway had more than a couple of the coloured erasers in their hands. It even looked like a few people were trading with each other.

'Can't wait till *that* fad is dead,' I said.

'Oh,' Faith said sadly. She reached into the front pouch of her hoodie and pulled out a bright blue eraser. 'I actually got you one.'

Faith got me a gift? If I told my parents that, they'd totally make fun of me for it, saying something like, 'Looks like you two are gettin' pretty serious!'

'I'm sorry,' I said smiling. 'I didn't mean it like that. They *are* cool.'

'Good,' Faith replied, smiling. She held the bright blue block out to me. 'I saw the blue one and thought you'd like it. Smell it! It even smells like blue raspberry!'

I held the eraser under my nose and took a big whiff.

'Huh,' I said. 'It really *does* smell like blue raspberry. How does Sebastian make these?'

'He probably buys them in bulk from somewhere,' Faith said, 'and then sells them at a higher price.'

The first bell went off. It was the warning bell, telling students they only had five minutes left to get to homeroom before school started.

Faith and I bumped fists and headed for our separate homerooms.

**Friday.
Homeroom.**

I managed to get into my seat just before the second bell stopped ringing. Zoe spun around and said, 'Something's not right.'

'You feel it too?' I asked. 'That whole thing with Jake is *still* bugging me.'

My cousin looked at me, confused. Then she pointed at the blue eraser I had in my hand. 'No,' she said. 'I meant that I could smell that eraser of yours. I thought you said you *hated* those things?'

'I did,' I replied. 'But they're starting to grow on me.'

Zoe's eyes narrowed. She paused for a moment, but then spoke confidently. 'Faith got it for you, didn't she?'

I laughed, nervous.

'Yeah,' Zoe said grinning. 'You're blushing. Faith gave that to you.'

'No, she didn't,' I said defensively, embarrassed.

Zoe paused again, watching my expression. 'She did. She's so into you.'

'Whatever!' I said. 'No she's not. She was just being nice.'

Zoe remained silent.

'Why?' I asked. 'Did she say something?'

'No,' Zoe said. 'But she doesn't have to. I'm a girl, I can read these kinds of things.'

Mrs Robinson stood up to make the morning announcements, but Friday announcements were always half-heartedly delivered. Brayden leaned over in his chair. 'You're still thinking about that stuff from yesterday?'

I nodded. 'Something about it feels off, doesn't it?'

'Like there's more to the situation?' Zoe asked.

'Exactly,' I said. 'Like it's unfinished.'

Brayden sighed. 'I think I'm going to have to side with Gavin on this one, buddy. You might be digging too deep, trying to find a story where there isn't one.'

I rolled the blue eraser on my desk, struggling to open my eyes because of how tired I was. 'You guys don't feel it?'

Zoe shook her head. Brayden did too.

'Are your ninja senses tingling?' Zoe joked. 'Look, you saved the day for like, the *sixth* time! I say, put that notch in your ninja belt and be happy about it. Seriously. It's Friday, the last day of the careers fair, which means today is basically a free day. None of our classes are gonna have any kind of work, and the last half of the day is just one big party. Isn't your mentor performing?'

'Yeah,' I said, sinking in my seat. 'He's got a bunch of his clown friends coming too.'

Zoe curled her lip. 'You might think it's lame, but I think it's super cool.'

Brayden chuckled. 'What if, instead of being a secret ninja, you were a secret clown? Training on your unicycle in some dark part of the school. No, wait, I just imagined that in my head, and I think that would probably scare the spew out of me.'

Zoe and I laughed.

Mrs Robinson finished the announcements just as the bell sounded. The students filed out of the room and onto the rest of their day.

Friday.
Right before lunch.

The rest of the morning was easier to get through as soon as I decided to forget about the nagging feeling I had. The careers fair was coming up, and I thought it'd be more enjoyable if my stomach wasn't rolling over itself from stress.

I saw Gavin outside the kitchen doors, standing in line for lunch, so I joined him.

'Hey,' I said.

'Howdy,' Gavin said. 'Good to see you're still in one piece.'

I laughed. 'Yeah,' but then I stopped. 'Wait, what? Why would I *not* be in one piece?'

'Because Jake is looking for you,' Gavin answered.

'No, he's not,' I laughed. 'Good one, dude.'

'No, really,' Gavin said, looking sombre. 'I saw him walking around the halls this morning asking about you. He even asked *me* if I knew where you were.'

'No, he didn't!' I said, desperately hoping that Gavin was playing a cruel joke on me. 'There's no way he's at school today, not after yesterday! How is he not suspended, or at least in detention?'

Gavin shrugged. 'Not every kid that gets in trouble is suspended. Some only get a slap on the wrist.'

'Jake got a slap on the wrist for stealing everyone's gum?' I asked loudly.

Gavin raised an eyebrow. 'I've got a few friends on the inside still,' he said, keeping his voice down. 'And they said there wasn't much evidence for Jake to get busted on. It was just that book bag and the note from the wolf pack. Jake's parents threw a fit because there wasn't anything that proved he was guilty.'

I slapped my forehead. 'Wasn't it enough that he confessed?'

'He didn't,' Gavin said. 'My sources said he never actually said he was the one taking all the gum. Principal Davis had no other choice but to let him go, and I understand why.'

'Because Jake might *not* have been the bandit,' I said, finishing Gavin's thought.

'Booya,' Gavin said. 'But I think it was pretty clear that Jake had *something* to do with it.'

The twisting feeling in my stomach returned. The idea that something was still wrong weighed heavily on me. Jake might not have been the bandit, but he was still a part of the bigger picture, but the problem was that nobody knew what the bigger picture was.

**Friday.
Lunch.**

I sat in the corner of the cafeteria, watching the doors like a hawk, waiting for Jake. From my spot, there was no way he could sneak up behind me. At least I hoped there wasn't – Jake *was* a member of the red ninja clan, and if anyone could sneak up on someone tucked into a corner, it would be them.

My neck started straining from sitting up so straight and pushing myself into the corner.

A couple of kids commented about how I was in 'timeout', but I hardly cared.

I could tell my eyes were drying out because

they would burn when I finally blinked. I was concentrating too hard on trying to see Jake before he saw me that I was beginning to feel exhausted. Bad news on top of the fact that I was already super tired from my lack of sleep.

My head started bobbing as students became blurry. Squeezing my eyelids shut, I shook my head wildly, trying to wake myself up. Every time I opened my eyes, my vision sharpened, and I could see everything again, but only for about three seconds before my head bobbed again.

Faces became blurs of colour, and voices became murmurs of nonsense, as a cold sweat chilled my body.

I set my head back against the wall and told myself it was okay to rest my eyes, at least for a couple of seconds. But when I opened them again, everyone was gone.

The cafeteria was completely empty. 'Great,' I said. 'I slept through the rest of the day!'

The lunch tables had been folded and pushed against the far wall, and all the rubbish bins had been lined with clean bags. The floor had been polished and gleamed like an ice skating rink.

I stood up, feeling a little upset that *nobody* had tried to wake me up, not even my friends! Zoe was gonna get an earful from me when I got home.

Walking to the double doors at the far end of the room, I heard the sound of something grinding along a hard floor. I spun around to see what was behind me, but there was nothing there.

The grinding came again, but this time from the hallway. Carefully, I walked to the tinted glass windows and peered into the lobby, but there wasn't anyone out there either.

At least I didn't see anyone *human*. A line of aliens floated down the hallway, winding down to a spot in front of the principal's office, where

erasers were being sold by a puppet that kind
of looked like Sebastian.

Strings were attached to Sebastian's hands
and head, pulling him back and forth, making
him dance. I looked up, trying to see who was
controlling the puppet, but the thread
disappeared into the shadows.

I watched a transaction take place, as one
of the green aliens handed the puppet version
of Sebastian some gold bars in return for a
bright blue eraser. The alien giggled like a
kindergartener, and then popped the eraser
into its mouth.

'Sick,' I whispered.

'Chase?' a voice asked from behind me. Chills ran down my spine.

The voice came from the cafeteria – the *empty* cafeteria! There wasn't anyone in there a few seconds ago! I had been alone!

'If it isn't Chase Cooper, as I live and breathe!' the voice said again, apparently recognising me.

I slowly turned, pushing my hands into my pockets to hide the fact that they were trembling.

The first thing I noticed was that the roof had suddenly disappeared and I was standing under a blanket of stars against pink and blue colours of the galaxy.

... what?

A man stepped forward, his face beaming. A black overcoat was draped over his shoulders and covered a white dress shirt underneath, along with a big white bowtie. The coat stopped short in the front but stretched out behind him, almost touching the back of his knees. The man looked like he was from an old-fashioned movie.

'Lovely night, isn't it?' the man asked, looking at the stars. 'The weather is *perfect*.'

I wasn't sure how to respond, so I just hummed. 'Mmm...'

The man paused when he saw my face. He stopped and held his hand toward me. 'You *are* Chase Cooper, aren't you?' his voice boomed.

I nodded. 'Who're you?'

The man put his hands out, and then pointed to his smiling face. He didn't say anything, trying to make me guess who he was.

I stared at him and finally shrugged my shoulders.

Again, he smiled, but this time bigger, and then pointed at his face another time.

'I don't know, dude,' I said. 'Do you work here?'

The man stood up straight and sighed. 'It's *me*! James Buchanan!'

'Ohhhhhh,' I said, leaning my head slowly back. I looked at the empty cafeteria under the twinkling stars. 'So I'm dead then. I died. My afterlife is going to be spent in the empty hallways of Buchanan School while James Buchanan tries to make small talk with me.'

JAMES BUCHANAN

James jumped back and put a hand on his chest. 'Am I … *dead*?'

'Only by a few hundred years,' I replied. 'Hate to break it t'ya.'

Buchanan walked over to the stage and took a seat. He leaned forward, resting his head in his hands. 'Dead,' he said softly in disbelief.

I walked up to the stage, feeling sorry for the old man.

Suddenly, he jumped forward with his hands up. '*Boo!*'

A very *not* manly sound escaped my mouth as I hobbled backwards and fell to the floor.

James jumped up and pointed at me like an immature child. '*Burn, sucka!* That's for making my mascot a *moose!*'

I had never felt more confused. '*What?*'

James spun in a circle with his palms facing up, and then spoke like he was a surfer. 'C'mon, *bro*,' he said. 'Look at the ceiling! It's gone and you can see stars! You really think you *died*?'

I stopped. 'This … am I *dreaming*?'

Suddenly, fireworks erupted in the sky.

'Boom!' he said, clapping his hands. 'You're dreaming, and I've been dead for hundreds of years!'

I remembered all the times I thought the ghost of James Buchanan had been messing with me. 'Are you haunting the school?'

James raised an eyebrow. 'Are you serious?'

'No,' I said, immediately, '... sorta.'

'No,' James said, opening his eyes wide. 'This is all in your head.'

'But why?' I asked.

'You probably fell asleep during lunch,' James said, taking a seat on the stage again.

I hopped up next to him and watched the line of aliens out the door. On the floor where I had been standing, giant puzzle pieces appeared. They were scattered out of place.

'Got any gum?' James asked.

'No,' I answered.

'No matter,' James said, pulling out one of Sebastian's pink erasers.

I shook my head and joked, 'Even if I did, the bandit probably would've got it by now.'

'Ahhhh, yes, the *bandit*,' James sang. 'Whatever came of that?'

I decided to give in and talk to James like he was a real person. Maybe it was part of my brain trying to talk to me, who knows?

'The bandit was caught. At least, I *think* he was caught.'

James raised his hand. 'Start *before* that.'

'Oh,' I said. 'Someone dropped a bag of stolen gum by my feet and—'

Shaking his head, James said, 'Before that.'

'What, like the beginning of the week?'

James nodded.

I took a deep breath. 'It all started on Monday. Some kids got their gum stolen. I thought it was strange because it wasn't just *one* kid, but a whole bunch of them, and *only* gum was taken.'

Two of the puzzle pieces on the floor connected clicked into place.

CLICK.

'Go on,' James said, furrowing his brows as he listened intently.

'So I wanted to help find the bandit, but none of my friends did,' I said.

'But you *did* get help,' James added.

'I did,' I sighed. 'Wyatt offered to help.'

A third puzzle piece slid across the tiles and attached itself to the other two.

CLICK.

'And to Wyatt, you said...' the president's voice trailed off.

'I said no at first.'

'At first?'

'Yeah. Wyatt and I aren't exactly besties, if you know what I mean.'

'Surprisingly, I do,' James joked. 'So what made you team up with him?'

I thought about it for a second and remembered the boys' locker room. 'Well, the bandit tried to frame me for stealing everyone's gum on Tuesday. He filled my gym locker to the brim with stolen gum.'

Another puzzle piece attached itself to the group.

James nodded, staring at the stars. 'And that's when you decided to team up with Wyatt?'

I shook my head. 'No,' I said, trying to remember. I stared into the pink and blue clusters of galaxies overheard. It was beautiful. 'There was a red ninja wristband sitting on the bench behind me when I slammed my locker shut!'

CLICK.

'Right,' James said. 'And you know how secretive and protective Wyatt is when it comes to his red ninja clan, don't you? There's no way *anyone* in the red ninja clan would leave a wristband like that lying around. Red ninjas are experts at covering their tracks, right?'

CLICK.

'Wyatt *wanted* me to find it,' I whispered, surprised that I hadn't seen the clue before. 'So I would remember that he wanted to team up. He *needed* me to get scared about the stolen gum in my locker so that when I saw the wristband, I'd want *his* help!'

James smiled, shooting a thumbs up at me.

'But the *second* bag of gum...' I said, realising the truth as I said it. 'That happened *after* I told Wyatt that I was done searching for the bandit! He must've... he *did* it to scare me again, didn't he?'

'Perhaps. But to scare you into doing what?' James asked. 'The first time he used fear to team up with you. The second time, he used fear to...'

A few more pieces slid in place on the floor, but there were nearly a dozen left sitting out in the open.

'To bust Jake,' I said. 'Wyatt kept on telling me that Jake was behind the theft, but *why* would he want to bust Jake?'

I watched the floor, hoping that another piece would move, but it didn't.

'That's the bajillion dollar question, isn't it?' James asked, chomping off one of the corners from the pink eraser.

It was one of those moments when you know you're dreaming and something weird happens, but at the same time you're like, of course that happened. It makes perfect sense that James Buchanan would take a bite out of one of Sebastian's erasers. And of course his breath would now smell like watermelon.

The remaining puzzle pieces trembled, like there was a brontosaurus stomping around outside.

I stared at the half-eaten eraser in the president's hand, and I remembered that the alien in the hallway *also* took a bite. My head started hurting as I tried to make sense of exactly what I was seeing.

James threw the rest of the eraser into his mouth, chewing it annoyingly.

'The *erasers*...' I whispered.

A puzzle piece slid into place.

CLICK.

The president blew a bubble until it popped.

'... are *gum*,' I said finally.

Fireworks erupted again in the galaxy above.

On the tiles below us, the puzzle pieces started moving, taking their correct place.

CLICK. CLICK. CLICK. CLICK.

My vision blurred as I stared at nothing, speaking quickly. 'The erasers are Sebastian's product, right? The school is selling them through the Pit! Kids are going nuts over them, but not because they're collectable erasers!'

CLICK.

'*But because they're gum!*' I exclaimed. 'They're not *scented*! They're *flavoured*!'

CLICK.

'Gum isn't allowed in school, but Sebastian found a way to sell it without the school knowing!'

CLICK.

'But what about Jake?' I asked.

The final puzzle piece connected, and I knew the answer.

'Sebastian is in cahoots with the red ninjas,' I said. 'It's *brilliant*! Sebastian gets the red ninjas to steal everyone's gum so that *nobody* has any, and then he sells it through the school so that *his* gum is the *only* choice they have! The staff were so fooled that even *they* were handing out free gum that they *thought* were erasers! This is what Sebastian has been working on for the past couple of months!'

I stared at the puzzle on the floor. The image that it created was a kitten howling at the moon. 'Um,' I said, confused. 'What's the deal with the howling kitten?'

James shrugged his shoulders. 'I dunno,' he mumbled. 'It's *your* subconscious.'

'You should know,' I said, 'since you're *part* of my subconscious and all.'

James grinned a sinister grin. 'Are you sure that I am though?'

The stars began spinning overheard, shining brighter. Each drop of light grew larger until they were blobs, too bright to look at.

I tried to cover my eyes with my hands, feeling them burn under my eyelids, but by the time I reached my face, the light was gone and I found myself staring at Faith's face. Is that what they mean when they say someone was a sight for sore eyes?

'Was it werewolves?' Faith asked, flashing her phone in my eyes. 'Were the werewolves chasing you again?'

I sat forward groggily, realising I was back in the cafeteria. My friends were huddled around me.

Reaching into my pocket, I pulled out the bright blue eraser Faith had given me. Without thinking twice, I took a bite out of it.

My friends all freaked at the same time.

'*Sick!*' Faith said, gagging.

'What's *wrong* with you?' Zoe asked, covering her mouth.

Naomi raised her eyebrows and nodded, impressed.

Gavin chuckled. 'Nice.'

'Blue raspberry,' I said, smiling with bright blue teeth. 'This *isn't* an eraser. It's a chunk of blue raspberry bubblegum.'

'Are you serious?' Zoe asked, lowering her voice. 'These erasers are gum?'

Gavin's jaw nearly hit the floor. 'Those things are everywhere!'

Naomi looked over her shoulder at the students in the cafeteria. 'Which is exactly what Sebastian wants, isn't it?'

I stood up, smiling at Naomi. She got it. She immediately understood what was going on. She was a good ninja, and I was glad to have her on my side. 'The howling kitten puzzle comes together for you too.'

'What?' Naomi asked, looking at me like I was crazy.

'Nothing!' I shouted, embarrassed.

As my bad luck would have it, my loud voice got the whole cafeteria to look at me, including President Sebastian.

'There he is!' I said, stepping forward, but stopped when I saw Jake and his wolf pack standing directly next to the president. 'Whoops.'

Sebastian snapped his fingers and the wolf pack followed orders, dashing across the cafeteria towards me.

All I could think about was that my friends were standing around me and I'd never forgive myself if any of them got hurt. So I started sprinting across the lunchroom.

Jake and the wolf pack were tearing their way towards me. The crowd of students and mentors was thick enough that they couldn't get to me quickly.

My nap must have lasted longer than I thought because most of the career mentors had already arrived and were setting up their display tables. I slid across the table where Gavin and Brayden's mentors were setting up.

As I landed on the other side,
I snatched a bundle of rope with a carabiner
from Gavin's rock-climber mentor.

'Hey!' he shouted.

'I'll bring it right back!' I said. 'Promise!'

Bursting through the cafeteria doors,
I slowed down to look behind me. Jake was
closing in, running at a full sprint. The
principal's office was barely five metres away.
If I had time to think about it, I totally
would've run in there, but instead I decided
that using the zombies in the library was
somehow the smarter decision. Don't judge me.

Swinging the rope over my shoulder, I jogged to the doors of the library, weaving my way around the students hanging around outside the doors. Lunch wasn't over yet, so inside the library, smarties were still zombified.

Pushing the handle down, I slipped into the monster-infested room.

Inside the library, it was cold and silent, like *creepy horror movie* silent. As I tiptoed across the carpet, I heard the faint sound of buttons clicking away along with the low buzzing sound of vibrating phones.

I hid behind a short bookshelf and snuck out to the centre of the room. On top of the bookshelf at the very end was a cluster of colourful balloons floating silently. Someone must've got them for a birthday or something.

On the other side of the shelf sat the zombies I was so afraid of. I could hear their heavy breathing as they stared at their phones, updating statuses or watching unbelievably cute kitten videos.

At the very centre of the room were two

staircases that joined halfway up to the second floor. It was much darker up there, and all I could see were the shadows of students, slouching at their tables, frantically typing messages.

The door to the library burst open. Most of the zombies didn't notice, but I heard a few grunt out of curiosity.

Jake stepped into the library. Only two members of his pack trailed behind him, sniffing at the air, hunting for their dinner. They knew people called them a wolf pack and thought it was funny to actually *act* like real wolves.

Scooting to the end of the bookshelf, I turned the corner. I had been in the presence of the library zombies before, but it wasn't a sight I'd ever get used to.

Kids sat at massive tables, staring into their phones, breathing out of wide-open mouths.

With faces glowing, they were hypnotised by whatever was on their five-inch touch screens, but still half-aware of the real world around them in case they needed to share their funny video with anyone who seemed remotely interested.

That was how their disease spread. That was how you got infected. Zombies infected by viral videos. *Viral.* Do you get it yet?

'Split up,' I heard Jake whisper.

His two wolves snorted their response.

I slowly pressed my back against the end of the short bookshelf, keeping as quiet as possible. Any sudden movements, and I'd be zombie food. I shook my head, feeling dumb because I thought the library was a good escape plan.

One of the zombies peeked over the top of his phone.

I froze, watching his eyes scan the top of the bookshelf. *'Please don't see me,'* I mouthed. *'Please don't see me.'*

The boy's phone blinked at him, vibrating in his hand. 'Rrrrrrg?' he groaned. 'Cute kiiiiitty.'

I exhaled, thankful to still be alive. Leaning to my right, I glanced down the aisle to see how far Jake and his wolf pack were from me, but they weren't there. I turned my head to look down the other aisle.

'Rarhg!' a zombie growled, right in front of

my face. It was the same zombie that had been looking for me only seconds ago. He pointed his phone at me, and murmured, 'Check out this video of a baby panda sneezing! You'll *die* from cuteness!'

I tried rolling to my side, but the zombie grabbed my shirt and started whining. 'C'mon, man,' he hissed. '*Pandaaaaaas.*'

With all my strength, I freed myself from the zombie's grasp, but soon realised he wasn't alone. Hobbling to my feet, I saw that the other library zombies were stumbling out of their seats, pointing their phones at me.

'Not good,' I said.

Jumping onto the short bookshelf, I sidestepped back down the aisle, careful not to lose my balance. And then I saw Jake and his wolf pack at the foot of the staircase. They turned when they heard all the noise too.

'There!' Jake shouted.

The two members of his wolf pack started sprinting through the room, dodging the zombified kids.

The crowd was much thicker where I was standing. Zombie hands reached toward me like long tree branches. I kept my vision straight ahead so I wouldn't accidentally catch a glimpse of some viral video.

And then I stopped, feeling a light bulb switch on in my head. *Use your surroundings!*

I pulled myself on top of the short bookshelf and grabbed the small bundle of balloons. If TV and movies have taught me anything, it was that someone could hang onto the strings of helium-filled balloons and float away to safety!

Snatching the strings that were attached to the brightly coloured balloons, I held them at my side. 'This has been a blast, but it's time for me to catch some air!'

Everyone in the room paused for a moment, staring at the balloons in my hands.

Pressing my lips together, I shook the balloons in my grip. 'Anytime now.'

The zombies looked at one another, confused. A few of them had even started recording me with their phones.

I CALL THIS ONE,
"MOVIES HAVE LIED TO ME."

I cleared my throat, pretty embarrassed. 'So *that's* not something that actually happens,' I said, releasing the balloons.

As everyone watched the helium-filled balls float to the ceiling, I jumped down from the bookshelf and had another idea. I might not have been able to use the balloons as my surroundings, but I could use the *zombies* to my advantage.

216

Pointing at the two members of the wolf pack, I shouted, 'Those guys haven't seen that sneezing panda video! Oh my god, can you *believe* it?'

All the zombies turned at once.

'Dude, you gotta see it! It's the funniest thing ever!'

'After you watch that, you gotta see this other video that's even funnier!'

'Yeah, man, those pandas are silly animals, but you ain't seen nothin' till you see the one with the kitty playing a keyboard!'

I expected the wolf pack to stop chasing after me, but they didn't even slow down.

I jumped off the bookshelf. When I hit the floor, I took the rope off my shoulder, keeping one eye on the zombies and one eye on the wolf pack.

Weaving the rope around one of the solid table legs, I looped it back around and connected the carabiner to the other side. I ran through the crowd of kids until I made it to the front desk, where surprisingly, a woman was sitting and reading a newspaper like nothing was out of the ordinary. She even looked bored!

'You got a book you want to check out?' she asked with a nasally voice, chewing her gum loudly. Funny how teachers are allowed to chew gum.

'Uh,' I said. 'No, not today.'

She waved her hand at me without looking up from her newspaper. 'Then scram, kid. Can't you see I'm a little busy?'

'Sorry, ma'am,' I said politely as I turned around.

The two members of the wolf pack were getting closer so I had to act fast. Pulling the rope tight, I looped it around one of the desk legs that the librarian was sitting at, and then I ran back *into* the crowd of zombies, yelling, 'Check out this video I found of a *manatee* wearing a *ninja* mask! *What were you thinking, manatee?* That mask doesn't even *fit* you!'

My plan was that the zombies would chase after me and trip on the rope, creating a wall of fallen kids between me and the wolf pack.

Then I would simply walk out of the library untouched.

The zombies began mumbling loudly as they turned toward me, desperate to see a manatee in a ninja outfit, which actually made me snort when I thought about it. Could you imagine that? A big ol' manatee decked out in ninja gear, sliding across the ice?

I shook the distraction out of my head, realising the wolf pack was too close for comfort. I sprinted towards the front doors of the library again, doing my best to keep the zombies at a safe distance, but I had underestimated their desire to see a ninja manatee and they were gaining on me.

'Let me see that manatee,' growled a zombie as she shot her hand out toward me. *'Ninja manateeeeeeeee!'*

I spun around to keep her from grabbing my shirt, but her fingers scratched my face.

'Gah!' I said. 'You guys are serious about your viral videos!'

I staggered backwards, about to fall over, but

thankfully I was at the front of the library where I had pulled the climbing rope across the ground.

From the corner of my eye, I caught a glimpse of the rope coming up. I tried stepping over it but it caught the back of my foot. I was the first kid to trip my own trap.

I hit the carpet hard, feeling it burn my elbows, and then I felt the weight of a hundred kids on me as they tripped on the rope. The floor shook like an earthquake as more kids joined the pile.

I gritted my teeth, expecting to be covered by the zombie tidal wave, but actually found myself sliding further *away* from where I had tripped. Since I was right at the front of the wave, I was getting pushed out.

Finally, I came to a stop at the entrance of the library. I stood up, brushed myself off, and looked at the hoard of kids lying on the floor. The members of the wolf pack were lying in the middle of the mess, groaning in confusion.

'*What. The. Heck,*' the librarian said sternly

from her desk. I'm pretty sure I could see a vein throbbing in her neck. '*What the heck?*' she repeated, holding both hands over her hair like she was keeping herself from pulling it out.

It was when her eye twitched that I decided to slip out the door quietly.

Out in the hallway, the other students were going about their afternoon without a clue of the mini zombie apocalypse that had taken place in the library.

Principal Davis's office was across the lobby, but before I could start moving, the door to the library swung open and Jake burst out.

'You've been nothing but trouble!' Jake shouted, trying to tackle me.

I tripped across the short hallway just outside the lobby as kids stopped what they were doing to watch. I'm sure they were hoping for a fight, but I wasn't going to give them a show.

Jake leapt onto my back as he tried to get me to fall over, but I kept my balance. I'm sure that to everyone else, it looked like I was carrying him on my back.

The cafeteria doors were right in front of me, which was the direction I was *trying* to fall in, but instead, I ended up losing my footing next to the doors that led to the costume department behind the stage.

With a painful thump, I fell into the backstage entrance. Jake tumbled over on top of me while I rolled across the dark room. I heard the wooden door click shut behind me.

My stomach sank, knowing that I was now alone in a room with Jake. I was dead meat. I was so dead they were gonna have to have a funeral for my ghost.

'Chase?' a voice asked from the corner of the dark room.

I picked my head up to see how this school was going to kick me while I was down. On the far side of the room, sitting at a dressing table, was Miko. He was in the middle of putting on his make-up.

I was started to say something but stopped when the shadows around Miko moved. Some were short and fat, while others were long and spindly, stretching nearly five metres off the ground. I wasn't sure what it was, but it was easily one of the scariest things I've ever seen in my life. And trust me, I've seen my share of scary things. Mostly in the dark pit of my locker.

'What's going on here?' Miko asked flatly.

Jake rolled to his back. His eyes opened wide as he scrambled to his feet.

'Mind your own business, clown!' he said, his voice shaking with fear. It was obvious that he was trying to sound like he wasn't scared. 'This idiot crossed the wrong kid, and he's gotta pay for it!'

Miko's eyes narrowed as he nodded, fully understanding the trouble I was in. He stood up and folded his arms.

The shadows behind him moved again, and slowly walked forwards into the light. They were Miko's friends, dressed in their clown gear. The tall spindly shadows turned out to be other clowns on stilts, hovering above everyone with their painted red smiles, but nobody was laughing.

Jake held out his shaking fist and squealed, '*I said stay out of it!*'
It's good to know that it's impossible for a bully to be a bully to everyone. It didn't matter how cool or how tough Jake was

to the kids at school, Miko wasn't going to have any of it.

'This kid bothering you?' Miko asked me, staring into Jake's soul.

'He's trying to keep me from exposing the school president, who's been stealing from students!' I said.

Looming over everyone, a clown on stilts honked his horn, but only once and slowly, making a *hurrrrrrrrr* sound that eventually died out.

I felt like I was having a fever dream.

Jake spun around and started moving toward the door, but a few of Miko's friends had already blocked off both exits in the room, one to the lobby and the other to the cafeteria. With stern looks upon their faces, they shook their heads at him.

Taking quick gasps of air, Jake stumbled backward. 'No,' he whispered. 'I can't be here. Not with *clowns*!'

'Then it looks like *someone's* in the wrong schoolyard,' Miko said. I think he was curling his lip, but his huge red lipstick smile made it hard to be sure. Miko looked at me. 'Get outta here, kiddo,' he said. 'We'll take care of your friend.'

The clowns blocking the entrance to the cafeteria stepped aside and opened the door, allowing me through. I took one last look at Jake, who was glaring at me so hard his eyes looked like they were glowing.

'This ain't over, Chase,' he hissed. 'Not by a long shot.'

I smirked, stepping into the cafeteria.

The careers fair had just started, and I could see Principal Davis standing with a huddle of other teachers all the way across the room. I was only about fifteen metres away from finally being free from this disaster! All I had to do was reach the principal without getting into any more trouble.

That's when I saw Sebastian in the aisle next to me. We made eye contact, and then he snapped his attention at Principal Davis across the room and then back at me. He did this a few more times – rapidly looking back and forth between the principal and me.

The president took off running as fast as he could down the aisle. I flinched, unsure about what to do, but then bolted like I was competing in a shuttle run.

Sebastian was taller than me, with long legs that made his sprint look easy. The gap between us widened. It was everything I could do to just keep up.

Students dove out of the way when they realised I was shredding down the aisle at full speed, but I still shouted to warn them. *'Move, move, move!'*

I kept my eyes forward, but could see that I was passing Sebastian. His heavy panting was falling behind me.

Principal Davis was getting closer and closer as I struggled through the cramp in my side.

This was it. I was going to tell Principal Davis the whole story, and nobody was going to stop me.

Slowing myself in front of the Principal, I tried talking, but my throat was so dry that I could only choke out a cough.

The principal turned towards me. 'Are you okay?' he asked.

Suddenly someone gripped my arm and pulled me aside. I tripped over my feet, stumbling away from the principal. I looked up into Wyatt's face.

'*What are you*—' I started.

'Just watch,' Wyatt interrupted. He pointed at the principal.

Principal Davis was still looking at me when Sebastian slammed into him at full speed. Both of them fell through the huddle of teachers until they smashed against the brick wall with a sickening thud.

The principal shook his head, and looked at Sebastian.

'Are you okay?' he asked, genuinely concerned. 'What happened? What's going on?'

Sebastian stood up immediately, speaking at light speed. 'Chase is lying! The gum I sell in the Pit is *good* for the school!'

The principal stared at Sebastian, clearly shocked.

Sebastian was panicking and kept running his mouth.

'It's *good* for business,' he continued. 'Even *you* said the added money in the budget was a good thing! Sure, I might've got a couple of kids to do the dirty work of stealing gum, but that was totally necessary! And yes, my erasers are blocks of bubblegum, which really isn't such a bad thing when you remember how much *money* I've made – I mean, the *school's* made.'

The cafeteria fell silent as Sebastian spoke like his volume was stuck all the way up.

'Gum isn't allowed at this school, alright?'
Sebastian said, waving his arms at the students
in the cafeteria. 'And I will *not* stand by and
watch students sneak gum into class! If they
want it, they'll have to *buy* it from me, through
the Pit!' Sebastian paused to catch his breath.
He turned to Principal Davis. 'So whatever
Chase said doesn't even matter! The gum is an
investment in *our* school's future.'

'Chase didn't say *anything* to me,' Principal
Davis said flatly.

'Um,'
Sebastian said,
staring into
space with wide
eyes. He must've
been replaying
his confession.
'Uh-oh.'

SEBASTIAN'S "UH-OH" FACE.

With a cold stare, Principal Davis put his hand on Sebastian's shoulder and escorted him to the end of the cafeteria. It was over.

I took a breath, savouring the victory, and then started to walk toward the principal. Wyatt grabbed my arm again.

'Let go, will ya?' I said, annoyed.

'What do you think you're doing?' Wyatt asked.

'I'm gonna tell Principal Davis everything I know,' I replied, yanking my arm away from Wyatt. 'Sebastian just confessed, so it's probably best if I'm there with my side of the story too.'

Wyatt paused, his evil grin stretching across his pale face once again. 'You think Principal Davis is going to listen to you? After all, you were *part* of Sebastian's scheme.'

My face grew hot. 'What are you talking about?'

Wyatt snickered. 'Don't forget the box of Sebastian's 'erasers' you delivered to the front office on Tuesday.'

My stomach dropped. Wyatt had given me

that box to deliver to the staff as a sign of faith. 'You set me up!'

'Of course I did!' the leader of the red ninjas said. 'I need some extra dirt on you to make sure you keep your place at the bottom of the food chain. So if you say anything, I'll remind Principal Davis of your *special* delivery.'

My fists were so tight that my palms started to burn. 'This was all part of your plan,' I said.

Olive stepped up and took Wyatt's hand. She stuck a piece of gum in her mouth, and then snickered. 'Hey, babe.'

Wyatt grinned.

Olive glared at me. 'Wyatt's gonna be the new *president*,' she said.

The room started spinning as I realised Olive was right. Since Wyatt was the vice president of Buchanan, he was next in line for president if something happened to Sebastian. And the way Principal Davis looked as he spoke to Sebastian made it obvious there was *no way* that kid was still president.

Wyatt stepped onto one of the lunch tables

and cleared his throat. 'Ladies and gentlemen,' he said. 'As your new *president*, I'd like to be the *first* to tell you that—'

'Not so fast!' Principal Davis said from the side of the cafeteria. Sebastian was in the hallway, waiting with a hall monitor as the principal walked towards Wyatt. 'This isn't like the actual presidency.'

Wyatt jumped off the table.

'There's clearly something fishy going on,' the principal continued, and then he gestured to the careers mentors scattered around the room. 'But since there are guests in the school today, it'll have to be sorted out first thing on Monday morning.'

Wyatt walked past me, bumping my shoulder. Olive was attached to his other hand as they marched back to their table. Wyatt was fuming. Good thing Principal Davis put him in his place, or else everyone would have to take orders from *President Wyatt*. Gross.

I took a deep breath. Even though things were still shaky, everything seemed under control again. My friends joined me at one of the tables.

'Um,' Faith said with a cocked eyebrow, 'so that was the craziest thing I've ever seen.'

Brayden leaned forward. 'At least Wyatt's not president,' he said. 'Can you imagine? Wow. Just... *wow*.'

'There was a second where I thought he *was* going to be president,' I said. 'What do you think's gonna happen to Sebastian?'

Gavin answered. 'Stripped of the presidency for sure, but nothing much after that. Slap on the wrist, maybe.' He looked at Zoe. 'This might call for another election, y'know.'

Zoe laughed. 'Fun! Election *weeeeeeeeek!*' she sang.

'So is Wyatt really that much of an evil genius?' Naomi asked, bringing the room down again.

'What do you mean?' I asked.

'I mean, Wyatt had a master plan this entire time,' Naomi said. 'A master plan that was *behind* Sebastian's master plan. Like, we know

Wyatt and the red ninjas were working with Sebastian for the past month.'

'Longer than that,' Brayden said.

'But the entire time that Wyatt was taking orders from Sebastian,' Naomi continued, 'he was actually figuring out his own plan to become the president. He figured out how to weasel his way to the top! And he'd been playing you – both of us – all week!'

Everyone nodded.

'He had his sights set on Jake the whole time,' Naomi said, chuckling in disbelief. 'Wyatt *needed* Jake to take the fall so he wouldn't have to. If the vice president of the school got caught stealing gum, he would get fired.'

'That's why he was so pushy about making sure we knew Jake was responsible for the stolen gum,' I said.

Faith sunk into her chair. 'He really *is* a genius.'

Zoe folded her arms. 'The good news is that he's *not* the president,' she said. 'So we can all sleep soundly tonight.'

'Jake was just a pawn this whole time,' I said, and then suddenly remembered he was with Miko. 'Wait a second … *what happened to Jake?*'

At that moment, all the kids in the cafeteria burst out with laughter. They were pointing at something near the front of the cafeteria, but I couldn't see what it was through the crowd of students.

The sound of a clown's honking horn bounced off the walls as my friends and I made our way to the front.

CLOWN JAKE

There, sitting on the edge of the stage, was Jake, leader of the wolf pack, member of the red ninja clan, quarterback of the Buchanan Moose football team … and he was painted up like a circus clown.

'We didn't make him do it,' Miko said, suddenly standing behind me as if he'd materialised out of nowhere. 'He offered to do it.'

'He *wanted* you to paint his face?' I asked.

'Yep,' Miko said. 'He said he would walk out of the room in a clown outfit if we left him alone.'

'What were you *going* to do to him?' Naomi asked.

Miko laughed. 'Absolutely nothing! We were just going to let Chase get a head start so he could make it to the principal without getting hassled!' Miko spun around and scanned the room. 'Looks like you took care of business too, kiddo.'

'Thanks,' I said. 'Hey look... I'm sorry for being hard on you this week.'

Miko raised his hand. 'No big deal. I get it from everyone.'

'You're a super cool dude,' I said. 'You do what you do because you love doing it, even when dorks like me give you a hard time for doing it.'

'It's all about shutting the dorks out, right?' Miko joked. 'I'm sure you have to do that all the time when you're parading around as a ninja.'

My jaw dropped and my friends gasped.

'How did you know?' I asked.

Miko just smiled like he was hiding a secret, and then winked at me before walking away.

'That dude is good,' Naomi said.

My friends hung around after Miko left. We joked about the tough week it had been and made fun of each other for a bit. I was the one they were picking on the most, but I didn't mind. The way they were goofing on me made things feel normal again, like we were just a group of kids with normal sixth-grader problems.

The cafeteria began buzzing with activity as everyone went on with their normal careers fair routine. Funny how quickly things settle down, even after a weird confession is screamed across the entire room by the school's president.

Another week at Buchanan and another bully busted. A ninja might not take breaks, but this ninja does. It's not easy getting through a week like that without anyone getting hurt, but I managed to do it. And that's a pretty impressive ninja skill, if I do say so myself.

Zoe, Brayden, Gavin and Faith returned to their seats. Naomi stood by my side. This week was the most time I've spent with her, and even though she was a good ninja, I learned that she was an even better friend. She never left my side, not even when things got tough. Actually, *especially* when things got tough.

'Thanks,' I said.

Naomi looked at me. 'For what?'

'For sticking by me,' I said. 'It means a lot to me.'

Naomi slugged me on the shoulder in the exact same stinkin' spot that Zoe had a couple of days ago. I did my best to keep from flinching, but the only way I could do that was to force a smile and squeeze my eyes shut.

Naomi laughed. 'Sorry about that,' she said.

'I'm just ... I'm bad at responding to compliments. What I *meant* was ... don't mention it. You don't need to thank me for being your friend.'

Just then, I felt a tug on my elbow. I turned, expecting to see Wyatt again, but it was a short boy who I only recognised from the hallways.

'Hi?' I said, making it sound like a question.

The boy didn't say a word. He handed me a folded note and briskly walked away, as if he were afraid.

'That can't be good,' Naomi sighed. 'What is it with kids at this school and notes? Why doesn't anyone communicate with their mouths, *like normal human beings?*'

'Right?' I asked, opening the sheet of paper. The writing on the note was typed, which somehow made it feel creepier.

You've crossed the line this time and have awoken a sleeping giant. You have been warned. The storm is not coming ... it's already here.

—The Scavengers

You've crossed the line this time
and have awoken a sleeping giant.

You have been warned.

The storm is not coming...
it is already here.

- The Scaveng

'Wonderful,' I whispered. 'I guess the
Scavengers *are* real.'

Naomi spun around so fast that she almost
tipped over. Frantically, she scoured the room.
'The Scavengers? Did you seriously just get a
note from the *Scavengers*?'

I scanned the cafeteria for the boy who
delivered the note, but he was nowhere to be
seen. Crumpling the sheet of paper in my hand,
I glanced at my friends who were only a few
tables away. 'It sounds like more of a warning.'

Zoe looked up from the group and waved at me to come over. I took a deep breath and exhaled slowly.

The Scavengers might've been the real deal, but there was no way they were going to take this victory away from me. I tossed the note into one of the rubbish bins along the wall as I started walking toward my cousin.

'You're just going to throw that away?' Naomi asked, jogging to catch up, still keeping an eye out over her shoulder.

'Why not?' I replied.

'I … because …' Naomi paused. 'Huh. You're right. Why not?'

'Their message was delivered,' I said. 'But I don't care.'

'You don't?'

I shook my head. 'Not today at least. We just won a huge victory over Sebastian and Wyatt, and I'd like to savour that for the rest of the day. I think I deserve that. I mean, I think *we* deserve that, don't you?'

A smile appeared on Naomi's face. 'You know, I think you're right.' She wagged her finger at me and spoke again. 'I *knew* there was a good reason you were the leader of the ninja clan. Too bad it's taken me this long to figure it out though. Maybe next time you can be wise a little *quaster.*'

'Mwah hahaaaa, very funny,' I said.

Once we got to our table, I took a seat between Faith and Zoe. Naomi sat on the end of the bench next to Brayden. Everyone was smiling except for Naomi and me.

Part of me wanted to tell my friends about the note from the Scavengers, but a bigger part of me was glad they didn't know. They could at least enjoy the rest of the day without the stress of new threat looming over their heads. That bad news could wait until later.

I took one more look behind me, just to make sure there wasn't anyone there. Y'know, like maybe another kid with a note, or a member of the red ninja clan, or one of the

Scavengers, or the fifteen president of the United States, or even the white ninja.

Man, Buchanan School was a *stressful* place. I shook the strange feeling from my shoulders and forced myself to smile – you'd be surprised at how *making* yourself smile has the power to brighten your day, even if it's just a little bit. And I had plenty of reasons to smile. No matter how crazy my life was, there wasn't anywhere else I'd rather be than in the cafeteria with my best friends.

Faith tapped my hand with her finger. 'Everything okay?' she asked softly.

'For now it is,' I said with a smile.

Diary of a 6th Grade Ninja Series

Collect the SET!

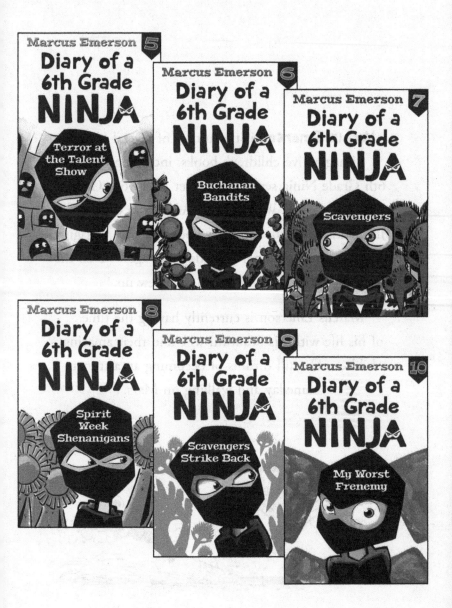

Marcus Emerson is the author of several highly imaginative children's books, including the 6th Grade Ninja series, the Secret Agent 6th Grader series, *Lunchroom Wars* and the Adventure Club series. His goal is to create children's books that are engaging, funny, and inspirational for kids of all ages – even the adults who secretly never grew up.

Marcus Emerson is currently having the time of his life with his beautiful wife and their amazing children. He still dreams of becoming an astronaut someday and walking on Mars.